MW01641657

K9 PARTNER

DORRANCE
PUBLISHING CO
EST. 1920
PITTSBURGH, PENNSYLVANIA 15238

Dorrance Publishing Co
585 Alpha Drive, Suite 103
Pittsburgh, PA 15238
Visit our website at www.dorrancebookstore.com

ISBN: 978-1-4809-3644-7
eISBN: 978-1-4809-3667-6

PROLOGUE

Westfield Police Chief Elmer Benson hung up his office telephone and stared straight ahead, deep in thought. Westfield Mayor Arthur Johnson had, as they like to say, "Ripped the chief a new one."

The mayor had indeed chewed out the chief. Chief Benson's secretary, Mary Carson stood in the doorway to the chief's office. "Mayor chew you out again, Chief?" said Carson, looking at the dejected police chief. "Yeah. Ripped me a new one. This crime wave is out of control." Chief Benson looked out of his office window. Mary Carson had been Benson's secretary for eight years. She knew when to back off. Ulmer continued to stare out his office window. He knew something had to be done, and it had to be done fast.

Westfield was a Mid-Western city of approximately 300,000 people. Its history was not one of a city with a preponderance for violent crime. It was a city where people did not lock their doors at night. But time had changed that feeling of security. Crime had taken an exponential jump over the last two years. Assaults, burglary, and white collar crime had spiked at an alarming rate. The citizens of Westfield were raising the roof to Chief Benson. His undermanned police force was doing all it could to stem the tide of crime. Mayor Johnson and the city council had adamantly refused to hire additional officers. Moreover, overtime was frowned upon. The Westfield Times likewise slammed Chief Benson. The situation had begun taking a toll on the 26- year police veteran. He decided to call a long-time friend for some advice.

Richard Nelson was the police chief in the town of Chancellorsville, 150 miles north of Westfield. Benson and Nelson had served together in the United States Air Force prior to joining their respective police forces. They served together as security policemen. Benson and Nelson frequently talked about their jobs, wives, families, etc. Nelson then asked Benson if he had received the police magazine he had sent the previous week. Benson replied that he had not - he was too busy with the increase in crime.

Benson reached into a desk drawer, where he had put the magazine. On the cover was a policeman in a crouched position. The officer had a leash attached to his right arm. At the end of the leash was a German Shepherd, teeth snarling! Benson read the article. He perhaps saw an answer to the burgeoning crime wave.

Chapter 1

Westfield patrol officer Randy Thompson sat in his police cruiser, reflecting on how things had changed recently in his hometown. He was well aware that the heat was on the Westfield PD. The steady increase in crime had the folks who call Westfield home walking on eggshells. Randy Thompson was born and bred in Westfield. He knew from a very early age that he was going to a police officer. When he was 34 years old, he had married his high school sweetheart, Susan Casey. Randy felt that he had a perfect life. His police officer salary provided a comfortable living for himself and Susan. Randy had graduated from Westfield High prior to obtaining an Associate's Degree from the local community college. He passed the Westfield Police Department screening process and academy with little difficulty. He was hired immediately. Randy could hardly contain himself as he began his Westfield Police Department career. That attitude and determination would serve him well as events were to unfold in Westfield. Now, as he snapped his mind to the present, the police dispatcher broke the quiet. "Westfield Dispatch to all units, reports of shots fired at 237 Walnut Street. All units respond. Code 5." Randy slammed his police cruiser into gear, turned on his lights, and headed for Walnut Street.

Walnut Street was located on the east end of Westfield. It was inhabited by the lower level of the economic strata in Westfield. A sizable percentage of the crimes were committed on the East Side. The recent increase in crime in Westfield had its roots on the East End. Crime had always been a problem on the East End. Most of the industry and economic strength resided on the

West and Northwest ends of Westfield. Randy Thompson and his fellow Westfield officers were very familiar with the residents of 237 Walnut Street. Richard and Bella Conley had resided at that address for more than 20 years. Both of the Conley's were well acquainted with a 12 pack of beer. With their two sons out on their own, Richard and Bella had filled their idle hours drinking beer and arguing. Randy was certain that Westfield police officers had responded to the Conley home at least six times.

Richard Conley had retired from the Westfield Electric Co-Op several years back. The idle time had not been good for Richard. At 63 years old, he felt emasculated. Bella had been the director of their household. She wielded strict control over all facets of the Conley family. Their two sons had long since escaped Bella's wrath. Richard frequently wondered how in hell he had put up with her iron -fisted rule.

Randy Thompson approached Walnut Street. He felt that he could drive to the Conley residence blindfolded. He could clearly recall the four or five times he had responded to 237 Walnut Street. He assumed that this response would mirror the prior responses. Randy Thompson would reflect on that thought process after this incident was cleared. He marked the time, 9:04 P.M.

Cops always complain about incidents occurring near the end of their shift. Randy's shift ran from 2 P.M. and 10 P.M. He was hoping that this incident would end quietly, and quickly. Unfortunately for Randy Thompson and his fellow officers, this response would take some time to sort out.

Two other Westfield patrol officers were already on scene when Randy Thompson rolled up on 237 Walnut Street. Sergeant Homer Edwards and patrol officer Ted Barnes stood by their police cruisers awaiting Randy's arrival. "Hey Sergeant, hello Ted. Conley's at it again?"

Edwards replied, "Yeah, and it's getting old. What is it about these people?"

Barnes, wanting to interpolate his own view, replied "Yeah, but I'll lay you odds that this will not be the last time we respond to this house."

Barnes had just finished making his comment when two loud, unmistakable gun shots rang out from the Conley residence. The three Westfield officers immediately took cover behind one of the black and white cruisers. Sergeant Edwards reached for his radio mike in his cruiser. He called in to

the Westfield police dispatcher, exclaiming, "Shots fired at 237 Walnut Street. Send additional units, fast!"

Edwards then directed Barnes and Thompson to safely reconnoiter to the sides of the residence and to hold fast pending other instructions. Additional units en route to 237 Walnut Street could be heard in the background. Sergeant Edwards decided to wait for reinforcements before developing and executing a strategy.

Sergeant Edwards directed the arriving units to fan out and instructed everyone in the 200 block of Walnut Street to stay indoors and stay away from windows in their homes. The sergeant then spoke to Westfield Police Department Lieutenant Robert Dawson via his black and white mike. Dawson asked Edwards if he would be able to handle the situation. "Yeah, Lieutenant, we have it under control," reported Edwards. Secretly, Sergeant Edwards thought to himself that the last thing he needed was that idiot Dawson running this situation. Edwards promised to keep the lieutenant abreast of happenings on Walnut Street.

Richard Conley did not respond when Sergeant Edwards attempted to reach him with a bull horn. Edwards decided that it was time to move. Before he could even begin to direct his officers, Conley shouted at the officer's from a second story bedroom, "Hey, you stupid sons of bitches. Why don't you give it a rest? My old lady and I are fine."

Sergeant Edwards responded, "Richard, why don't you lay down the gun and come on outside?"

"Kiss my ass," replied Conley. "Don't you boys have more important things to do?"

Edwards was unaware of the condition of Bella Conley. Whether or not she was alive posed a significant dilemma for Andress. Dealing with a lone, armed individual was difficult enough. This situation, however, was different. Richard Conley was well known to the Westfield police. Along with the roughly half dozen incidents, Conley had accumulated several public intoxication arrests, and two Driving While Intoxicated arrests. Benson wondered how this thug was not behind bars. Moreover, Edwards wondered what life was like for Bella Conley.

Edwards' and the Westfield police officers on scene were startled to see Bella Conley run out of the home. She ran as best she could towards the po-

lice vehicles on scene. When shielded safely behind the police vehicles, she told Edwards that Richard Conley was extremely intoxicated, armed with a revolver, and vowing not to come of 237 Walnut. Bella told the police officers, "He said that he was tired of dealing with cops and would take some of them with him."

Edwards observed Bella Conley. He felt bad for this woman, while also wondering how a woman like Bella could put up with that type of man for so many years. Nevertheless, with Bella safely out of 237 Walnut, the Westfield sergeant could now concentrate on getting Richard Conley under control.

Richard Conley remained holed up inside 237 Walnut. Edwards' endeavors to talk to Conley fell on deaf ears. Edwards had attended a hostage negotiator course several years ago. He continued attempting to make contact with Conley, without success. Edwards informed the officers on scene that, for now, they would wait. He did not want to unnecessarily expose police officers to danger. For the time being, they would wait out Conley. Edwards' approach to the standoff was in keeping with established protocol. Bella Conley was safe. Established procedures called for patience. Sergeant Edwards directed the Westfield police officers to stand fast.

Local news agencies monitoring their scanners responded in force. Edwards had officers ensure that they stayed out of harm's way. But just when Edwards thought it couldn't get any worse, the Westfield Police Department dispatcher informed Edwards that Lt. Dawson was en route. *Great*, thought Edwards. *Now I have to put up with Lt. Dawson s' interference.*

Dawson arrived and sidled over to Edwards. "Fill me in, Sarge." Edwards managed to hide his contempt while briefing the lieutenant.

Dawson immediately took charge of the standoff. "Listen, Sarge, I don't think we should wait on this guy. The longer we wait, the bolder they become." Edwards attempted to interject the procedures he had learned at the hostage negotiator course. Dawson cut him off. "Look, Sarge, we don't have time to apply those principles. We need to get that guy out of there. Fire tear gas into the house. Let's wrap it up."

Edwards reluctantly followed Lt. Dawson's directive. He ordered Thompson to fire tear gas into 237 Walnut Street. Edwards told Thompson to hold off with the tear gas until he made one more attempt with the bull horn.

"Mr. Conley," said Sergeant Edwards, "this is your final chance to end this thing. Lay down the gun and come on out. In two minutes we are going to fire tear gas into the house."

Edwards waited for approximately three minutes. When he determined that Conley was not going to come out, he directed Thompson to fire the tear gas into 237 Walnut. Edwards glared at Lt. Dawson as the projectile smashed into the living of the Conley home. People who have never been exposed to tear gas have no idea how overwhelming it is. A person not wearing a gas mask is simply not capable of remaining in a room when tear gas is introduced. Police are routinely exposed to tear gas. They are placed in a room wearing a gas mask. They then are required to remove the gas mask, state their name, date of birth, and badge number before again donning the mask prior to leaving the room. Police officers never forget the impact of tear gas.

The tear gas canister had the desired effect, and then some! The Conley residence was immediately filled with the caustic gas. Richard Conley had been holed up in the second story front bedroom. He quickly realized that he could not remain in his residence. His only option was to exit his home. Conley quickly descended the stairs of his residence, gun in hand. He hesitated at the front door, rubbing his eyes in an attempt to them.

The handgun in Conley's hands was a .357 Magnum. It is a very powerful handgun. Conley was very proficient with the .357. He regularly fired at a range outside of Westfield. The Westfield police officers braced themselves as Conley prepared to exit via the front door. Edwards instructed Conley to drop the weapon and put his hands in the air. Conley apparently did not hear the direction from Edwards, or more likely, ignored it.

Conley stepped onto the porch of 237 Walnut. Prior to dropping the .357, Conley, left-handed, raised his right hand to rub his irritated eyes. Edwards again ordered Conley to drop the weapon. He did not comply. The Westfield police officers saw an individual, highly agitated, refusing to comply with an order to drop his weapon. Conley stumbled, and lunged forward. That prompted several of the Westfield police officers to open fire on Conley, killing him instantly.

Bella Conley witnessed her husbands' death. She was hysterical. She tried to run to her mortally wounded husband. Westfield police officers restrained Bella Conley as she tried to get her already dead husband. Her hysterical

screams permeated the otherwise quiet night. Lt. Dawson stood up behind a black and white. He stared at Richard Conley's lifeless body. Dawson had been employed by Westfield PD for just over three months. He had been a police officer for 15 years. All of his police service had been with a small, rural force in Montana. He had never experienced a high-profile incident like the one that went down on 237 Walnut Street.

Sergeant Edwards quickly realized that Dawson looked as though he was in shock. He immediately took charge. He directed that officers secure the scene. This included having officers clear the external and interior of 237 Walnut Street. Emergency medical services arrived. They took immediate charge of Bella Conley. Edwards knew that they would have to interview Bella Conley. He also knew that it would be impossible to interview her until she regained her composure. It would definitely not occur here on Walnut Street.

Westfield Police Chief Ulmer Benson arrived on scene approximately 40 minutes after the incident culminated. All police departments, regardless of its size, notify the chief when an officer is involved in a shooting incident. Chief Benson approached Lt. Dawson. Dawson saw the chief approaching.

Benson asked Dawson, "What the hell went down here?" Lt Dawson attempted to brief the chief. Benson was well aware of Dawson's timid tendencies. The chief was also aware that Sergeant Edwards had actually commanded the Westfield police response to 237 Walnut Street. Benson waved Edwards over to where he and Dawson stood watching the Westfield police officers mop up the scene.

"Good job, Sergeant Edwards," said the chief. "Let's take a walk, Sarge."

Chief Ulmer Benson didn't mince words, a characteristic that was well known by all Westfield police officers. "Sergeant Edwards," said Benson, "why was it that you were running this incident?"

Edwards responded, "Chief, I can't speak for Lt. Dawson. I saw that he appeared to be confused. I looked at him several times, waiting for him to take the lead. He did not move. I took over."

Benson then asked Edwards to give him a play-by-play of this incident. Edwards briefed the chief on how the Westfield Police Department handled the standoff. The chief listened to Edwards' account of the standoff at 237

Walnut. Benson's frustration was evident. Chief Benson complimented Edwards on his handling of the standoff. "Sarge," said Chief Benson, "make sure that all of the I's are dotted and the T's crossed. I think this incident is going to generate some heat on us. Again, good job!"

Homer Edwards was sound asleep when his sleep was interrupted at 9:30 AM, the morning after the standoff at 237 Walnut. He had climbed into bed at 4 AM. Chief Andress" secretary, Mary Carson, informed Homer that he needed to beat feet to the station. The mayor and chief needed to talk to him ASAP! Homer jumped into the shower wondering, of all things, how Lt. Dawson fared with the chief. He would soon find out.

Chief Benson and Mayor Arthur Johnson were waiting for Sergeant Edwards. "Come on in, Sergeant Edwards," said Chief Benson. Mayor Johnson approached Edwards and extended his hand. "Great job last night," he said. The mayor then handed a copy of the Westfield Times to Edwards. The banner print read, "*Westfield Man Shot by Police.*"

"Sergeant Edwards, the heat is on. I've been taking it in the shorts over this incident." Mayor Johnson continued, "The city council, as well as numerous citizens, have been raising hell. They want to know why Richard Conley was shot by three Westfield police officers as he apparently rubbed tear gas from his eyes. What happened?"

"Mayor, it all happened so fast," said Sergeant Edwards. "We certainly gave Richard Conley ample opportunities to avoid what happened." Edwards continued, "I really felt that we could entice Conley into surrendering after his wife exited the home. Didn't turn out the way we would have liked, Mayor."

Mayor Johnson, his frustration showing, continued, "How can three officers interpret Conley rubbing tear gas out of his eyes as pointing his .357 at them?"

Edwards continued, "We did everything we could, strictly by the book. It's very easy for the citizens of Westfield, including the city council, to pick apart an incident. I back my men100 percent! Mayor, speaking for my shift, we're doing all that we humanly can to cut into the increase in crime."

Chief Benson then interjected his unsolicited opinion. "Sergeant Edwards is right, Mayor. We have been asking for much needed radios, computers, and vehicles. We are consistently asked to hold on, that things are going to improve. Truth be told, Mayor, it's always one type of delay or another."

Chief Benson then reached into his desk to retrieve a brochure that he was intending to show to the mayor. The chief handed the brochure to Mayor Johnson. The mayor looked at the cover of the brochure. On the cover was a police officer. A German Shepherd stood at the side of the officer.

The mayor seemed transfixed. He had seen TV accounts of police dogs, much like most citizens had. He had not, however, paid much attention to police dogs. Mayor Johnson did seem interested. "Tell me, Chief, have you looked into these police dogs? Do you think one of those police dogs could help us here in Westfield?"

Chief Benson didn't hesitate. "I have indeed. I can't believe we haven't looked into this sooner. I've talked to several of my friends. All of them said that they can't imagine not having at least one police dog on their force."

Mayor Johnson hesitated before instructing Benson to look into these canine police schools. Benson was to get back to the mayor ASAP. Prior to departing for his office, Mayor Johnson told Benson and Edwards, "I'll message the city council. Find out cost, location, etc. We have to let the folks of Westfield know that we are doing something to stem our growing crime spree."

Chapter 2

Westfield mirrored hundreds of cities across America. It offered its citizens the trappings and convenience of a major city, without the problems of cities like New York or Chicago. It had enjoyed a peaceful history. Although not immune to crime, it was thought to be free of the type of crime found in the major cities. Westfield police and the general population had, for approximately two years now, seen a significant increase in crime. Crimes like burglary, assaults, and most alarming of all, a significant increase in narcotics activity had the mayor, the Westfield police, and citizens concerned.

Chief Andress had pleaded with Mayor Johnson to hire additional officers. Moreover, the chief had requested funding for improved vehicles and equipment, like radio's and Tasers. Mayor Johnson had experienced a frosty working relationship with the Westfield City Council. The mayor was determined to get a handle on the growing crime, and specifically, gang activity.

Chief Benson wasted little time looking into police dogs. He, like most people, had seen police TV shows depicting how effective well-trained police dogs can be. The chief was well aware that observing police dogs on TV and understanding how they work were two very different things. He was able to locate a number of canine training outfits throughout the country. They all seemed to be reputable enterprises. Benson's interest was particularly piqued by an outfit located in Mobile, Alabama. Southern Training Academy specialized in training police, narcotic, and explosive detector dogs. Southern Training Academy was owned and operated by Harvey Rhodes, a retired United States Air Force (USAF) Security Police Master Sergeant. Rhodes had dedicated his entire 20 year USAF career to handling, training, and managing police dogs. His USAF canine experience included tours of duty in Vietnam, Alaska, and several stateside assignments. Among Rhodes' stateside assignments was a stint as Instructor, Department of Defense (DOD) Dog Center, San Antonio, Texas. Rhodes modeled the Southern Training Academy after the military programs.

Benson placed a call to Harvey Rhodes at Southern Training Academy. Rhodes provided Benson with a roundup of detailed explanation of the programs available, to include capabilities of a well-trained police dog, schedules, and of course, cost. Rhodes informed Benson that he would e-mail all of the pertinent information directly.

Benson printed the information immediately and looked it over before taking it over to City Hall. He was impressed with the Southern Training Academy in general, and with Harvey Rhodes in particular. Harvey Rhodes hailed from Philadelphia, Pennsylvania. He enlisted in the USAF in 1966. He was interested in an administrative career, much like "Radar O'Reilley" on the popular television series M.A.S.H. The reality was that the USAF assigned him to the military police field. After

boot camp and police school, the USAF assigned Harvey to a base in Florida. He quickly realized that he didn't much care for waving cars through gates and guarding airplanes. The base commander in Florida ordered the base police commander to acquire police dog teams to increase security. Rhodes immediately volunteered for the USAF Patrol Dog School, located at Lackland Air Force Base in San Antonio. Rhodes and several fellow USAF policemen journeyed to Lackland Air Force Base in May of 1967.

Chapter 3

The history of police dogs is fascinating and extensive. The Department of Defense (DOD) Dog Center is located at Lackland Air Force Base (LAFB) just outside of San Antonio. The USAF trains all military dogs for all four of the branches of the DOD. Although the DOD Dog Center opened in 1958, the history of dogs in police and security dates back to the caveman era. The DOD felt that young enlisted men and women should have a sense of the history of working dogs, much like aviators study the history of flight. Rhodes and his cohorts journeyed to Lackland AFB in the spring of 1967. They had no idea of the adventure waiting for them.

The Patrol Dog Course at Lackland ran for 12 weeks. Rhodes and his classmates, although excited about the pending program, were nonetheless nervous. The initial two days consisted of classroom work which included canine first aid, dog handling equipment, course objectives, and history. While very interesting, the fundamental information, like equipment, paled in comparison to history.

Harvey and his classmates were mesmerized listening to the history taught by the DOD instructors. Patrol Dog Course instructors told the class that drawings found in caves depict dogs in front of the entrance to the cave barking at animals. Historians theorize that the cave dwellers fed the dogs, who alerted them to the presence of animals or human enemies. Roman gladiators adorned dogs with spikes and chains. Those dogs were then trained to attack. The result was that the folks facing the Romans first had to deal with hundreds of dogs prior to actually engaging in battle. The DOD instructors next taught the class how Napoleon Bonaparte had his men agitated dogs, then chained them to the base of the Bastille forts. That tactic required his adversaries to deal with the dogs prior to surmounting the walls.

The instructors then moved on to 20th century use of dogs in modern warfare. Rhodes and the students were surprised to learn that the United States of America did not utilize dogs for any reason until May 9, 1942. Major countries like France, Germany, Russia, and Japan utilized thousands of dogs throughout World Wars I and II. Numerous breeds of dogs were used principally as guard and attack dogs. Japan was widely known to train what were referred as "satchel dogs." Satchel dogs were trained to attack enemy troops at varying distances. Those dogs were initially trained with dummy packs. During combat, timed explosive devices were attached to the dogs. When those dogs reached the enemy, the Japanese would detonate the charges. This tactic, although not widely known, was very effective for the Japanese. The reward for the dogs, said the instructor, was not good.

Harvey Rhodes and his classmates' interest and enthusiasm grew with each lesson. These lessons increased their understanding of this fascinating field. The two-day orientation concluded with the students chomping at the bit to meet their dogs and get started. That evening, Rhodes and his classmates were hanging around their barracks shooting the breeze. It was evident to Rhodes that enthusiasm would not be lacking with the new dog handlers. Dog handler students from senior classes razzed the rookie class, as they had been razzed during their initial week. One senior class member really laid on a heavy dose of BS about how dangerous it was to work with these German Shepherd dogs.

Rhodes and his class were told why the US DOD settled on the German Shepherd as the primary breed for sentry dog duty. Their instructor told them that many breeds are suitable for police/military duty. "However," said the instructor, "the German Shepherd dog is, in the opinion of all concerned, the most suitable, hands down." A classmate of Rhodes asked the instructor why, for example, the services didn't use Doberman Pinschers or Rottweilers.

"Good question," said the instructor. "Dobermans are unsuitable for military service for two specific characteristics: they can't work in cold climates. Moreover, unlike the German Shepherd, they will not bite and hold a person. Dobermans are a very high strung dog." Rhodes was once again mesmerized by the information proffered by the Patrol Dog Instructors.

DOD Instructors attempt to match new dog handlers by size and personality. A student standing 5' 6" would not be assigned a huge, 90-pound German Shepherd. Moreover, instructors endeavored to observe the new students during the orientation process. A student that is outgoing and boisterous would be matched with the most outgoing dog. It is not an exact science. Canine instructors possessed an uncanny knack of matching new handlers and dogs.

Rhodes and his classmates had, for the most part, a hard time sleeping the night before dog assignment day. The students had been informed that the DOD would pay up to $1,500 for a healthy German Shepherd. The DOD also accepted donated German Shepherds. Whether sold or donated, the dogs had to meet the following criteria: minimum 12 months old, weigh at least 55 pounds, and possess at least three of the four primary canine teeth. The DOD instructors were very up front about one fact: the majority of German Shepherds sold or donated were too aggressive to remain in society.

Dog assignment day finally arrived. Rhodes and his classmates arrived at the DOD kennels with hundreds of students at 0600 hours. The barking of anxious German Shepherds filled the morning air, adding to the rookie classes' anticipation. Rhodes' decision to volunteer for the canine program seemed even more exciting when he stood with his classmates observing senior students tend to their assigned dogs. Anticipation continued to build as the moment of truth approached. In just a few minutes Rhodes would meet his new partner.

Harvey Rhodes was one of the largest students in his class. At 6' 2", he carried his 210 pounds well. The instructors waited until all of the classes ahead of the rookie class had hit the field with their dogs. The rookies observed the German Shepherd dogs that would constitute their class. Rhodes looked over the dogs in row five, the rookie class assigned kennel. All of the German Shepherds were barking excitedly, as though they realized that something was about to happen.

The instructors began to assign dogs to the rookies. Harvey watched as rookie after rookie was matched up with the German Shepherd most suited to them. All of the dogs were assigned, save two occupying the last two kennels. Rhodes stood by nervously. The two remaining dogs could not have been more different. One of the dogs weighed approximately 80 pounds, the other closer to 100. The smaller dog was assigned to the final remaining student, leaving the larger dog for Randy Thompson.

The dog assigned to Rhodes had been sold to the DOD by a family in Columbus, Ohio. This 20-month German Shepherd was named Shadow. Rhodes was immediately captivated by Shadow. The Ohio couple, both in their 60s, did not want to sell Shadow. Their decision to sell was necessitated by one fact: Shadow's weight. Although usually possessing a friendly disposition, Shadow turned a full 360 degrees when any person dared to get close to the senior couple. DOD personnel involved in the procurement of German Shepherds look for that disposition above all others. The German Shepherd dog is, with few exceptions, at the very top of the protection pecking order. Along with the physical requirements, prospective dogs must display a consistent protective attitude – at all times. Shadow possessed all of the necessary characteristics!

Rhodes' instructors guided him through the introduction protocol, which principally involved letting the dog come to him. Rhodes was instructed not to stare at the dog, as that may be seen as a challenge. When Rhodes had established what the instructors considered sufficient rapport, they led him safely into the kennel. Shadow took an immediate liking to Rhodes. The big German Shepherd began to playfully rub up against Rhodes. This interacting quickly calmed Rhodes' nerves. The instructors realized that they had made a perfect match with Rhodes and Nero.

The following two days were devoted to what was referred to as "handler-dog relationship". The objective of this exercise was to allow the handlers and dogs to become comfortable together. Rhodes and his classmates were given detailed instruction on the critical importance of the handler-dog relationship. Rhodes' previous experience in Vietnam would prove useless in this situation. He could not recall any experience that even closely matched this training. With actual training about to commence, Rhodes and his classmates were sky high and ready to go.

The remainder of the initial week was dedicated to basic obedience training. The DOD instructors had emphasized the fact that, regardless of what it can do in police tactics, it must be trained to a near fail safe level of obedience. Rhodes discovered that even in the somewhat mundane area of obedience training, the program was well defined and systematic. Edwards was to learn that all facets of training were delivered in a systematic manner referred to as "shaping," or "successive approximation." Shaping and successive simply meant a teaching paradigm where dogs are trained in a manner designed to minimize confusion. For example, a dog must be trained to successfully demonstrate sit one step away from the trainer prior to teaching it to stay at two steps, etc.

The really exciting part of the program commenced in week two. Harvey Rhodes and his fellow students were about to embark on their journey into what was referred to as "controlled aggression." Controlled aggression is a process wherein dogs are trained to manifest aggression only when commanded to do so by the handler. The instructors did explain that their dogs would attack immediately if the handler was attacked.

The German Shepherd dog is a direct descendant of the wolf. Although conventional wisdom says that all dogs stem from the wolf, none resemble the wolf like the German Shepherd does. Although somewhat smaller than the wolf, German Shepherds nevertheless are very adaptable as pets and guard dogs. Rhodes and his classmates were taught that, of all its attributes, the German Shepherd's fierce loyalty sets it apart from other working dog breeds. Along with loyalty, the German Shepherd possesses phenomenal olfactory and hearing abilities. However, the most significant characteristic of the German Shepherd dog are what trainers refer to as the "42 reasons". The 42 reasons refer to the German Shepherds' teeth. Those teeth can deliver a composite bite of roughly 1,600 pounds per square inch (PSI). Rhodes' instructors shared with the class a number of training accidents wherein students had been severely bitten; some of those bites were almost life-altering. The instructors didn't mince words in explaining to the students the intrinsic danger involved in training police dogs.

Moreover, the instructors emphasized to the class the critical importance to listen to instructions and work together. Rhodes did all he could do absorb as much information he could.

Week two commenced with the instructors demonstrating attack sequences. The students sat mesmerized as they watched the instructor team put a German Shepherd through an attack sequence. They watched as the instructors guided the demonstration dog through a sequence of on-leash and off-leash attacks. Rhodes marveled at the control demonstrated by the instructor team. The sequences presented included scenarios on-and-off leash bites. The class watched closely as an instructor, wearing a leather/canvass sleeve, simulated the behavior of a criminal. The instructor handling the demonstration dog challenged the instructor portraying the bad guy. When the bad guy took off running, the dog handler immediately unleashed the German Shepherd. The German Shepherd caught up with bad guy in a few seconds. The bad guy had on his left arm a canvas/burlap sleeve that is able to absorb the incredibly strong bite of a German Shepherd. The students watched in awe as the dog tore into the sleeve worn by the bad guy. At a predetermined interval, the bad guy ceased moving the sleeve. The handler immediately commanded a loud, clear "out" to the dog. The students stared in awe once again as the German Shepherd immediately released the bite and return to the handlers' side. The dog handler then commanded the bad guy to stand and keep his hands in the air. The dog handler then commanded the bad guy to move forward to a point 10 to 12 feet in front of the handler/dog team. The handler then informed the bad guy that he would be moving forward to search him. The dog handler commanded the dog to "stay" as he moved forward. At a prearranged point, the bad guy would shove the dog handler. The only time a police dog is trained to attract without command is when his partner is assaulted. This exercise clearly demonstrated that tactic. The students once again watched in awe as the dog did not hesitate, attacking the bad guy once again. The handler once again called off the dog. The bad guy was unlikely to try to escape again.

The instructors then assembled the class for another skull session prior to having the class participate on controlled aggression training. The instructor team lead then addressed the class. "Listen people," he said to the class, "this is where we separate the men from the boys." He hesitated briefly before continuing, "Listen men, this a very critical point in your training. Make no mistake about it, these dogs are capable of inflicting life changing injuries. Your absolute attention is required." The lead instructor hesitated for effect before continuing. "Let me give you all a few statistics: The German Shepherd dog is capable of inflicting a devastating bite. The dog can exert a bite of approximately 1,600 pounds of pressure per square inch." The lead instructor then continued, "For comparison, however, a hyena can exert up to 21,000 pounds of pressure per square inch. Now that is a powerful bite!" The lead instructor concluded his comments by urging the class to listen closely to his partners. "There is an intrinsic danger when it comes to training these beautiful dogs to attack. Your undivided attention is critical." Harvey Rhodes and his classmates could not wait for controlled aggression training to commence.

The instructors had the handler/dog teams line up at 15-foot intervals with their dogs sitting at "heel". The heel position has the dog sitting beside the handler, facing forward. The handlers were taught to assume a suspicious, crouching posture while encouraging the dogs to "watch him" in a low voice. One of the instructors, wearing a protective sleeve, emerged from behind a cluster of bushes. The dogs immediately manifested a very noticeable change in disposition. The instructor approached the line of dogs in a crouching, menacing manner. With the dog handler's continuing to quietly tell their dogs to, "watch him, boy". When the instructor/agitator reached a point approximately 10 feet from the line of handler/dog teams, he commenced with loud, exciting movements meant to agitate the dogs. The tactic worked. Rhodes and his fellow students were astonished by the change in their respective dogs. Shadow nearly jerked Harvey Rhodes and several other students off their feet. Despite ample instructions from the instructors, the strength and tenacity of the dogs astonished the nascent handlers.

Shadow quickly bolted to the end of the leash. Like his classmates, Harvey Rhodes was unprepared for the strength of the large German Shepherd. The instructor /agitator ceased enticing the dogs by standing up and remaining motionless. The handlers then commanded their dogs "OUT", which was the command from the handler that directed the dogs to cease aggression. The handlers were quick to learn that the dogs were not always eager to let go of the agitator. This characteristic, along with the German Shepherds' fierce loyalty, became evident to Rhodes from the commencement of controlled aggression training. Rhodes, like countless dog handlers over many years, quickly discovered that the attachment between dog and handler is unmatched. Controlled aggression training advanced to a point where the handlers could command their dogs to attack off leash, bite the sleeve worn by the agitator, release the sleeve, and return to the handlers' side.

The instructors, satisfied with the class' performance in controlled aggression, introduced two additional tactics: building search and field scouting. The instructors briefed the class: "Men, it's time to introduce tactics wherein the dogs' olfactory capacity will enable you to locate fugitives or lost persons." The instructors explained to the class how dogs can easily detect a lost or hiding person. The instructor continued, "The human body emits an odor that is comprised of three molecular components: salt, water, and waste particles." The instructor then explained to the class that even after a shower, the human body nonetheless emits an odor. The instructor continued, "When searching for a fugitive, for example, you can rest assured that he or she is perspiring profusely."

Field scouting was the next tactic taught to the class. Rhodes sat with his classmates as the instructors explained how a dog can easily detect the scent of a human being at up to 300 yards. The lead instructor continued, "You were already taught about human scent. Those scent particles leave the body of the fugitive or lost person and fade away in what is called a scent cone. That scent cone is driven away from the quarry. The scent cone is affected by wind, humidity, terrain." The lead instructor asked if the class had any questions.

One of Harvey Rhodes' classmates asked the lead instructor to elucidate on the effect of wind, humidity, etc. "Good question," replied the lead instructor, "let me explain. Human scent is definitely influenced by environment. Rain drives scent particles to the ground, which may require the dog to get somewhat closer to the quarry. Wind affects the human scent by determining scent density, A gentle wind dissipates the human scent in into what is called a 'scent cone.' Stronger wind carries human scent away in a narrower cone. However, the human scent is stronger when the wind is high." Rhodes and his classmates were anxious to get to the field for scout training.

The instructors taught the class how to utilize their dogs' phenomenal olfactory ability to locate their quarry. Harvey Rhodes was blown away when Shadow led him directly to the location of one of the instructors. The instructors also taught the class how to utilize the wind to their advantage while field scouting. "You always want to give your dog his or her best chance to locate the quarry. Utilizing what is referred to as the down wind flank, or the bottom of the grid usually results in a successful search." Rhodes and his classmates quickly learned how each individual dog responded to the scent of the quarry. The instructors then had the quarry agitate when the handler team was about locate him. The handler/dog teams were able to quickly master field scouting.

Teaching the dogs to locate intruders hiding in buildings was the next tactic presented to Harvey and the class. The class was surprised to learn that field scouting and building search were similar in many ways. The instructors explained that human scent particles in buildings are affected by air conditioning systems, heating, windows, furnishing, etc. It is also subject to gravity. Building searches invariably involve flushing perpetrators from offices and warehouses. The class was told that perpetrators usually believe that they are safe from detection by hiding up high. They think a dog is incapable of picking up their scent from on high.

The exact opposite is the case, however. Human scent is extant; therefore, subject to gravity. The instructors explained to Rhodes' class that a systematic search of buildings commencing at ground level will invariably lead to uncovering the perpetrator. Rhodes and his classmates were introduced to a series of trials. Harvey Rhodes and Shadow excelled at building search. Shadow immediately shifted into search mode as Rhodes entered the vacant building, telling the dog in a suspicious tone, "Find him." Rhodes was able to easily follow Shadow as the big dog responded to a scent that seemed to come from heaven. The perpetrator was hiding in a second story closet. His scent had escaped the closet, drifted along a short hallway, and down a staircase. Rhodes encouraged Shadow as the German Shepherd pulled Rhodes up the stairs towards the fugitive hiding on the second floor. The dog led Rhodes directly to the closet and to the perpetrator. The instructors were pleased with the class regarding building search. Rhodes and Shadow were singled out as outstanding in building search.

The third and final olfactory tactic taught to Rhodes and his classmates was tracking. The instructor staff was quick to point out that not all German Shepherds track. They explained that approximately 25 percent of German Shepherd's track. "German Shepherd's," pointed out the lead instructor, "are scent-seeking animals. Their natural inclination is to keep their nose off the ground. They are inclined to keep their noses 'upwind' or into the wind."

The instructor continued, "For reasons unknown, one of four German Shepherds will utilize both the wind and scent particles deposited by the lost person or fugitive."

Once again, Harvey Rhodes and the class were introduced to another facet of canine work. They listened intently as their instructor continued, "The standard bearer for tracking is the Bloodhound. No one knows why hounds track the way they do. But rest assured, they will track you down every time. However, German Shepherds who track do it very well." The instructor explained that tracking is not a compulsory skill for police dogs. Police units, both civilian and military, identify the dogs in their units that track. Those handler/dog teams respond when a fugitive or lost person incident occurs.

The instructor then went into an explanation of what occurs in a tracking situation. "You guys remember when we taught you about human scent? Well, tracking is distinguished from scouting by how the dog locates the quarry. In field scouting, the dog seeks airborne scent. In tracking, the dog follows scent left by the quarry that clings to the vegetation, bushes, etc. The combination of perspiration and butyric acid leave a trail for the handler/dog team to follow."

The instructors then explained the steps taken by the handler to induce the dog to track. German Shepherds that are inclined to track are taken to a point where the fugitive or lost person was last seen. The handler was taught to point to the spot, or perhaps trail, in question, where he commands the dog to track. The handler encourages the dog, particularly when the dog displays interest. The handler would continue to encourage the dog to track. If the dog lost interest or hesitated, the handler would gently but enthusiastically encourage the dog to pick up the track. The instructor taught Rhodes and the class how to navigate obstacles like streams and paved roads. The class was taught, for example, that if the dog tracks a fugitive or lost person to a running stream, that they were to cross to the other side in an endeavor to reestablish the scent. The same process would allow handlers to reestablish the track should a fugitive or lost person cross a road.

Harvey Rhodes and his classmates were then presented with various tracking trials. Shadow was one of the class dogs that took to tracking with alacrity. The lead instructor made it a point praise Rhodes and Shadow.

"Rhodes, you have an outstanding tracking dog there. You should do well in tracking situations." Harvey Rhodes was absolutely thrilled with Shadow. They excelled in all facets of training. He was convinced that he would do quite well with Shadow.

Harvey Rhodes went on to have a stellar USAF career in the canine field. When he retired, he realized that working the dog program was in his blood. He decided at that time that he was going to operate a professional dog training academy. He committed himself to developing a first-rate canine academy. He was determined to provide the same quality training that he had received so many years ago.

Chapter 4

Six Westfield officers volunteered for canine duty. Chief Benson interviewed the six officers after reviewing their "jackets". All six of the candidates had exemplary records - all seemed worthy. The chief selected Randy Thompson to attend the canine course at Southern Training Academy. He spoke to Randy and Sue Thompson after announcing his decision. "Randy," he said, "we are really counting on you. Mayor Johnson and the city council are behind you. I really had to lobby for the funds. I'm counting on you to justify the dog. Do us proud, Randy."

Southern Training Academy was located just north of Mobile, Alabama. Harvey Rhodes had located his training academy in the Southern part of the United States to ensure year-round training. Rhodes had saved money, and along with several investors, developed a state of the art kennel/training facility. Randy Thompson was very impressed with the Southern Training Academy. He could hardly contain his enthusiasm. Rhodes then took Randy out to the kennel to meet his new partner.

The big German Shepherd stood in his kennel eyeballing Rhodes and Randy. Black with strands of silver, the big dog weighed approximately 90 pounds. "Randy," said Rhodes, "say hello to your partner, Nero." Randy Thompson squatted down in front of Nero's kennel. The big dog stared at Randy before moving to the rear of the kennel. Nero's insouciant demeanor did not discourage Randy. He was absolutely enthralled by Nero. Rhodes informed Randy that Nero had been purchased from a dog breeder in Michigan. Nero weighed 88 pounds and stood 26 inches at his shoulders. He was what was referred to as "moderately aggressive". Rhodes explained that moderately aggressive indicates that a dog possesses a balance between its aggression level and trainability. Harvey told Randy that Nero had passed all the physical and psychiatric traits so necessary in police dogs. Moreover, Rhodes ensured Randy Thompson that connecting with Nero would be easy. "We'll have a skull session in the morning prior to getting more acquainted with the dogs."

Randy Thompson and his fellow students were acquainted with their respective dogs following a two-hour introduction. He was to experience the same course and material and program Rhodes and his fellow students did so many years ago. Rhodes related his experiences with his dogs to Randy and his classmates as the course progressed. Randy bonded exceptionally well throughout the Southern Training course. Nero excelled in the entire course curriculum. He even excelled at tracking, a skill not compulsory for police dogs. The course concluded with Randy Thompson and Nero by garnering honor grad laurels. Randy and Nero returned to Westfield. Randy and Sue Thompson had spoken daily while he was out of town. Sue did her best to keep him current. Despite her best efforts, Randy Thompson had no inkling of what lie ahead!

Chapter 5

The Westfield crime spree had spiked exponentially during Randy's absence. Burglaries, assaults, drug abuse/sales, to name a few, were out of control. Suffice to say that Mayor Johnson had not been sleeping well. Benson and Johnson had arranged a press conference/demonstration with Randy and Nero for the very next morning. Randy was anxious to demonstrate Nero's skills. Moreover, Sue Thompson was also thrilled to witness what her intrepid husband had learned. The Westfield Times, local TV stations, and local radio stations were waiting when the man and dog of the hour walked in. The reporters and visitors were stunned when the handler/dog team walked in to Mayor Johnson's spacious office. Most were dog owners. Those dogs ranged from Poodles to Great Danes. None, however, were anywhere as impressive as Nero.

The mayor thanked everyone for coming. He quickly introduced Chief Benson, who said, "Ladies and gentlemen, today marks a significant day here in Westfield. This officer, Randy Thompson, and his magnificent partner, Nero, are going to have an immediate impact on our growing crime rate. Randy, why don't you give the folks here a brief rundown on Nero's capabilities." Randy proudly stepped to the microphone, Nero closely by his side. He briefed the folks regarding the Southern Training and it's rigorous training he and Nero had received. The audience and news agencies were thrilled when Randy introduced Richard Nelson, the Chief of Police of Chancellorsville, and their canine handler, Bob Walsh. Nelson and Walsh had driven over from Sommersville for the occasion. Walsh would act as agitator for the show and tell.

The entourage moved outside to a small park across the street from Westfield City Hall. Randy proceeded to put on an on-and-off leash obedience demonstration for the audience. Nero performed flawlessly all of the basic obedience commands: sit, stay, down, etc. The large German Shepherd was a stunning specimen. The audience was impressed; they were anxious to see the big dog perform the police tactics that they hoped would take a bite out of the raging crime spree. They were about to see!

Bob Walsh, the Sommersville police dog handler appeared from behind a tree. He was wearing a sleeve comprised of burlap. The audience was not aware that under the burlap, Walsh was also wearing a canvas "gauntlet". The German Shepherd is capable of easily ripping through the outer burlap and inflicting significant harm to a person's arm. Military and civilian police department dog handler's, with very few exceptions, are painfully aware of the injuries suffered by handlers and fugitives. Harvey Rhodes had been forthcoming in providing Randy Thompson and the remainder of the class with graphic examples of injuries suffered by dog trainers and handlers. Rhodes told the class that handlers had lost fingers, toes, calf muscles, and testicles. Randy snapped back to the present. It was time to show what Nero could do.

Randy and Nero performed flawlessly. Sue Thompson thought that her heart would burst through her chest as she watched her husband and Nero run through a controlled aggression session. The big dog demonstrated the clear ability to attack, cease attack, and remain still while Randy searched the "perp".

Sue and the audience were most impressed by the final tactic, the standoff. A standoff is the part of controlled aggression wherein the dog handler demonstrates absolute control over the police dog. Officer Walsh commenced the standoff exercise by running towards Randy and Nero. At a predetermined point, Walsh turned and ran away from the handler/dog team. Randy ordered Walsh to halt. When Walsh failed to heed the command, Randy unleashed Nero, who took off after Walsh, who was approximately 70 yards away. The agitator then gave up, stopping and throwing his arms above his head. Randy, after observing that the bad guy had given up, immediately called off the big dog, who immediately stopped and returned to Randy's side. The standoff exercise thrilled the audience. Sue Thompson again thought that her heart would burst with pride. The demonstration cemented the mayor's decision to involve a canine team to help stem the crime wave engulfing Westfield. The mayor and citizens would not have long to realize the efficacy of their decision.

Chapter 6

Chief Benson, following the advice from Harvey Rhodes, developed a special shift for Randy and Nero. Instead of working a standard 2 PM – 10 PM or 10 PM – 6 AM, Randy and Nero would work an 8 PM – 4 AM shift. The theory behind this schedule would enable Randy to utilize Nero to assist two shifts during the peak hours for crime in Westfield. Randy was enthusiastic about his new schedule. The canine team would work Wednesday through Sunday. Sue Thompson was not particularly thrilled at the prospect of her husband working weekends. She did not complain, however, because she realized that it was a great career opportunity for Randy.

Chief Benson had briefed the entire Westfield Police Department on the impending arrival of Nero. Randy did not know what to expect from his fellow officers. He expected the barking and howling he would receive from the rank and file. Chief Benson asked Randy to brief each shift regarding the capabilities and limitations of a well-trained German Shepherd police dog.

Randy and Nero commenced their first night of patrol duty shortly after 8 P.M, on a cool, breezy Wednesday. Chief Benson decided to give Randy and Nero the run of the city. The chief did not want the handler/dog team confined to a particular sector. The shift sergeants were instructed to allow Randy a period of time to acclimate Nero to his new working environment. The Westfield police officers working the 2-10 P.M. shift would quickly learn of Nero's capabilities.

The Westfield Police Department had customized a black and white sedan for Randy and Nero. The front passenger seat was removed and replaced by a padded platform that enabled Nero's head to remain level with Randy while on patrol. Randy experienced a prodigious sense of pride as he hit the streets with his partner. The folks downtown did double takes as Randy cruised around downtown Westfield. Many of them had seen police dogs on various TV cop shows. Observing a Westfield police officer with his dog was quite another thing.

Randy and Nero had patrolled the four sectors of Westfield for 90 minutes when a call from the dispatcher piqued Randy's interest. The dispatcher notified all Westfield police officers that a potential domestic violence situation was in progress on the West Side. Randy's mind flashed back to the incident where Richard and Bella Conley's argument resulted in his death. Randy wondered if he had had Nero, would Richard Conley be alive today?

Several Westfield units were on scene when Randy arrived. The situation was starkly similar to the Conley incident. Randy held back with Nero, unsure of how his fellow officers would react to their presence. The on-scene sergeant, Bill Blakemore, was known as a take-charge guy who demanded loyalty and obedience from his officers. The wife of the man holed up inside had escaped her husband's clutches. She told Blakemore that her husband had been beating her on a regular basis for years. She also informed Blakemore that he had several guns inside their residence.

Randy approached Sergeant Blakemore, who was running the operation from his black and white patrol vehicle. Randy spoke to Blakemore, "Hey, Sergeant, what can I do to help?"

Blakemore grunted before telling Randy, "Stand by, Thompson. I'll let you know if I need you and your animal." Randy had been warned to expect some hesitation, or even resentment from the rank and file. Blakemore monitored the situation from behind his cruiser. Like the Conley standoff several months ago, the strategy was to wait out the individual inside the two-story home. Blakemore, a 44-year-old, 17-year veteran of the Westfield Police Department, was very cognizant of the fallout several months ago with the Conley incident. Blakemore endeavored to coax the husband out of the house with a loud holler. When several minutes passed with no response from inside the home, Blakemore grumbled to no one in particular, "I guess we'll have to use tear gas to flush him out. Let's make certain the we don't shoot this one."

Randy hesitated before mustering the nerve to say to Blakemore, "Sergeant Blakemore, maybe Nero and I could flush him out." Blakemore stared at Randy, prior to responding, "Stand-by, Thompson."

Blakemore then called Lt. Dawson, the milquetoast shift commander, to get his approval for tear gas. Dawson then asked Blakemore if the handler/dog team was on scene. When Blakemore replied that they were, Dawson instructed that the handler/dog team be utilized prior to tear gas.

The human body constantly emits an odor that consists of three basic molecular components: salt, water, and waste particles. Those particles are extant. They are subject to wind if outdoors, and subject to gravity indoors. Dogs possess a phenomenal olfactory ability. Numerous studies conducted over the actual distance a dog can detect human scent. Dog handlers are seldom caught up in how far away the quarry is; they just know that their dogs have picked up human scent.

Police officers vow to "protect and serve" on the surface. Nevertheless, cops never hesitate to put another feather in their caps. Randy had been prepped by Harvey Rhodes that some police officers resent the notoriety attached to canines. He knew that he had to give Randy a shot at flushing out the disgruntled husband who still refused to demonstrate an inclination to exit the house.

"OK, Randy, the brass wants to give you a shot. What do you need us to do?" Randy, his adrenaline rising, replied, "Sarge, get on the loud speaker and tell him that he has ten minutes to exit the house. If he fails to do so, a police dog will be sent in to flush him out." Blakemore gave the individual one more chance to exit the house. He did not! After a ten-minute wait, the sergeant instructed Randy to go for it.

After cautiously arriving at the front door of the home, Randy announced in a loud and authoritative voice, "I have a trained police dog! You must exit the building immediately. If you fail to do, my dog will be unleashed. You may be bitten." Randy waited for another moment or two, then unleashed Nero.

The irate individual had taken to the attic, surmising that the dog would be unable to locate his position in the house. The individual did not know anything about human scent and how it is subject to gravity. Nero proceeded to perform a systematic search of the main floor of the home. Randy followed close behind the big dog as he covered the entirety of the first floor. Randy prepared to send Nero up the staircase to the second floor. He once again warned the individual that a police dog was about to ascend the stairs to the second floor. Randy waited for approximately one minute prior to sending Nero up the stairs to the second floor.

Nero quickly cleared the second floor. Although the big dog did not respond to the individual specifically, he did, during the search of the second floor, display a mild interest in the ceiling. Randy had already developed enough confidence in Nero's mannerisms to understand that the quarry was hiding in the attic of the home. Randy reached down to quietly pet Nero, who was by then definitely showing intense interest at the stairs leading up to the attic. Randy then announced to the individual hiding in the attic, "I have a trained police dog. If you do not come down immediately, the dog will be sent up to subdue you. I will wait one minute." The minute expired with no indication from the individual that indicated he would surrender.

Randy's adrenaline reached a fever pitch. The potential for violence notwithstanding, he wanted to ensure that his initial exposure with Nero to be a success. His concern was about to be put to bed. Randy opened the door to the attic staircase, commanding Nero to "find him, boy". The big dog had already locked on to the scent of the individual. The angry man had hidden behind several boxes of clothing. Randy kept Nero on leash. He feared that he would not be in a position to protect Nero should the individual open fire.

Randy's mind flashed back to his training with Harvey Rhodes at the Southern Training Academy. Rhodes had urged the class to "Always study your dog closely. You will find that your dog can differentiate between a training exercise and a real-life situation." Randy could see that Nero was particularly keyed up as they headed up the stairs to the attic. As the handler/dog team neared the top step, an explosive sound shattered the stillness. The angry individual had fired two shots at Randy and Nero from no more than six feet away. The unsteady hand of the shooter prevented him from hitting Randy or Nero.

Randy did not have to command Nero to attack. The dog sensed that his partner was in jeopardy. It took the dog less than one second to launch himself at the man with the gun. The individual was in the process of rearming when Nero hit him chest high, knocking the weapon from his hand. The shooter endeavored to shield himself with his arms. It didn't help. Nero shredded the shooters' left arm and thigh before Randy holstered his revolver prior to pulling Nero off the individual. Randy praised Nero prior to commanding the shooter to fall to his knees and raise his arms.

Sergeant Blakemore and two other uniformed officers crept up the attic stairs. Blakemore shouted to Randy, who responded that the situation was "Code 4", which is the universal police designation that all is under control. Blakemore reached the top step of the attic stairs, then stared in astonishment at the scene that had unfolded in the attic. Blakemore asked Randy if he or Nero were hurt. "We're fine, Sergeant Blakemore. Guy took a couple of shots at Nero and me. He missed. Nero was on him in a second." Blakemore had the two uniformed officers search the shooter and take him from the attic. "Make sure we get him looked at by EMS," he ordered his men.

Blakemore spoke to Randy after the shooter was taken down from the attic. "Damn, Randy, great job."

"Thanks, Sarge," replied Randy. "All of the credit for this pinch goes to Nero. He was on that guy in an instant." Blakemore, Randy, and Nero descended the steps to the second, then first floors. Exiting the home to the front porch, they were surprised to see Chief Benson and TV reporters approaching. Randy lagged behind, not wanting the dog to be spooked after what had transpired 15 minutes prior.

Chief Benson, displaying a grin as big as Montana, approached Blakemore, Randy, and Nero. "Good job, guys," said Benson. The chief continued, "It looks like our investment was the right choice."

Randy stood off to the side, letting Blakemore bask in the limelight. It was not the first time that Sergeant Blakemore hogged the limelight. Chief Benson, however, was aware of Sergeant Blakemore's habit of hogging the credit whenever he could. The chief cut off Blakemore and approached Randy and Nero. "Randy," said the chief, "tell me in detail what happened." Randy Thompson related to the chief what had transpired in the attic of the home. The chief then asked Randy how he thought the incident would have played out without Nero. Randy responded that the chance of injury would have been exponentially higher without Nero.

Word of the incident spread like wildfire throughout the Westfield Police Department. Most of the comments were positive. There were, to be sure, a handful of officers who looked upon the handler/dog team as a threat to their chances for recognition. Randy returned to headquarters to accomplish the necessary paperwork. A number of officers stopped by to offer congratulations for a job well done. Randy and Nero finished the remainder of their initial shift without responding to another incident. Randy Thompson checked out at 4 AM. He was very satisfied with the first night out with Nero.

Word of the incident also spread throughout Westfield. Sue Thompson had answered a number of telephone calls in the morning while Randy slept. Mayor Johnson paid a visit to police headquarters to discuss the incident. His honor was effusive to everyone at headquarters.

"Good morning, Chief," said the mayor.

Chief Benson looked up from his desk to acknowledge his boss. "Morning, Mayor, thanks for stopping by. This place has been a madhouse this morning. Citizens and news agencies have been calling with questions about the incident." The chief continued, "Mayor, things could not have gone any better. Thompson and Nero were able to diffuse a situation similar to the Walnut Street incident. We really have added a valuable resource."

Chapter 7

Randy slept in until 3 PM the following day. Sue Thompson told Randy that she had answered no less than 15 calls from people offering congratulations for last evenings' incident. Two of the calls were from news radio and TV people. Randy explained to Sue that any contact with media personnel comes the Westfield Police Department Public Information Office. Randy told Sue, "The brass would have a fit if I talked to the press without permission." He continued, "I'll have to be careful in matters regarding Nero and the press."

Shift number two started quietly enough. Randy was fascinated by the interest Westfield folks showed in Nero. He quickly realized that riding patrol with a large, beautiful German Shepherd dog garnered many second glances from citizens. A surge of pride swept over Randy as he patrolled Westfield. He was given the run of Westfield; he and Nero were not confined to a specific zone. Chief Benson had instructed the shift sergeants to utilize Randy and Nero for any incident wherein the dog could assist in handling a situation.

Sergeant Bill Blakemore fell into the middle of the pack regarding the new addition to Westfield's attempt to combat the surge in crime. Police officers, particularly those with seniority, resented losing pinches to younger officers. They specifically had no interest in sharing kudos with a gimmick like Nero. Nevertheless, orders were orders. Blakemore and his fellow sergeants knew that they would catch hell from the chief for not utilizing the dog when they had a chance.

Bill and Mary Hamby were in their mid thirties. They were very fit, with a consistent exercise regimen. Along with exercise club memberships, the Hamby's program included a brisk three-mile walk six nights per week. Bill Hamby was President of the Westfield National Bank. He was a third-generation Hamby. His grandfather, Harold Hamby, had immigrated from Ireland following the Great Potato Famine. He landed a job as a bank teller at Westfield National Bank. His diligence, dedication, and demeanor caught the eye of bank officials, who quickly moved him up at the bank. Bill Hamby's father, Fred Hamby, had followed in Howard Hamby's footsteps at the Westfield National Bank, working his way up to president. Naturally, Bill Hamby followed his father into the banking field at Westfield National Bank. He was also very active in community affairs like the Boy Scouts of America and Special Olympics. Bill Hamby was a pillar of the community. The Hamby name was golden in Westfield.

Butch Richards was well aware of Bill and Mary Hamby. Richards had moved to Westfield approximately six months before the current crime wave. Originally from Boston, he had moved from Beantown to escape increased heat from local, state, and federal law enforcement. Richards had delved into a myriad of crimes: narcotics, prostitution, and grand theft auto to name a few. Richards had moved quickly to establish a new "enterprise" in Westfield. He knew that he would not be able to match the money he made in Boston. Richards was willing to take the drop-in money in order to avoid the heat. He reasoned that he would, in time, do very well in this one-horse town. Richards had quickly recruited a handful of thugs who were impressed by his bravado.

Butch Richards was extremely intelligent. Not one to waste time, he quickly learned who were the movers and shakers in Westfield. He had noticed that the name Hamby was frequently mentioned in the Westfield Times and on local TV. He spent considerable time observing Bill Hamby's routine, both at the bank as well as at home. Richards had survived in Boston by staying a step ahead of the cops and feds. He anticipated easy pickings in Westfield. He formulated a plan that would enable him to make a score, then perhaps move on to another hick town.

Bill and Mary Hamby were creatures of habit. It was like shooting fish in a barrel regarding the Hamby's routine. Richards determined that a kidnapping of the Hambys would be easy. The plan was simple: Richards and two other thugs would snatch the Hambys during their nightly walk. They would hold Mary Hamby until Bill Hamby went to the Westfield National Bank in the morning. He would be instructed to bring $500,000 in cash to a predetermined place. Richards decided that they would snatch the Hambys on a Friday, since the Westfield Police Department brass would not be working on Saturday. Richards surmised that he could collect the loot and split it with his two cronies before splitting from Westfield.

Bill and Mary Hamby set out on their three-mile walk on a brisk Friday evening. They usually set out around 9 PM, after the sun set. Their walk took them to the outskirts of Westfield. Butch Richards had scouted the Hamby's nightly routine. He determined that they would snatch the Hambys just south of downtown, then move them to a rented manufactured home a few miles south of town.

Randy Thompson and Nero commenced their patrol that Friday evening at 8 PM. Randy was becoming more and more relaxed as he and Nero settled into a routine. He had also begun to develop rapport with the citizens of Westfield. The people of Westfield had seen police dogs on TV shows like COPS. It was another thing to see one in person. Randy would drive around until he saw folks congregating; he would stop to let Nero to hike his leg. Many of those folks would cautiously approach the handler/dog team. Randy would caution those folks to remain at least ten feet away from Nero. He patiently answered their questions about Nero. One astute gentleman asked Randy if he felt that Nero could put a dent in the crime wave. "Yes, sir, I really believe we can."

Bill and Mary Hamby were settling into a groove. By 9:15 they had settled into a brisk pace. They reached the south end of Westfield, where they were most vulnerable to any nefarious individuals. Bill Hamby was a very cautious person. He always approached life's challenges with a positive, upbeat attitude. Bill knew that the southern part of Westfield was the area of town where they were most vulnerable to trouble. His awareness always heightened during their walks. Bill and Mary had no idea of the terror they were about to experience.

Butch Richards and his cronies hid themselves in a vacant lot on Pine Street, adjacent to a warehouse. The lighting was poor at best, traffic very light. Bill and Mary Hamby rounded the corner at the intersection of Pine Street and Jackson Avenue. The time was 9:25 PM. Butch Richards and his cronies pounced on the Hamby's before the couple knew what hit them. Richards and another thug took Bill Hamby to the ground as two others easily overpowered Mary Hamby. They were hauled off of Pine Street and dragged to the rear of the vacant lot. The Hamby's hands were tied behind their backs. Their mouths were gagged. Richards and the others loaded the Hamby's into the bed of Richards' pickup truck. Richards had decided to deviate from the normal practice of kidnapping the bank president and family and holding them at their home pending the banker going to the bank to retrieve cash. The Hambys were childless. Thus, he knew that they would not be missed overnight.

Chapter 8

The trio transported the Hamby's to the manufactured home without incident. The bank president and his wife were put into an unfurnished bedroom. They remained bound and gagged. Bill Hamby endeavored to calm his wife as best he could, given the circumstances. But despite his endeavor to calm Mary's fear, she looked paralyzed. He knew that a high percentage of these kidnappings do not end up well. He determined that he would somehow find a way out of this predicament. He castigated himself for being so careless with Mary's safety. His trepidation grew exponentially when Butch Richards entered the bedroom. He looked at the Hambys with contempt in his eyes and said, "Okay, Mister Bank President. Let me tell you what is going to happen. You, Mister Bank President, are going to your bank when it opens at 9AM tomorrow." Richards paused for effect before continuing. "Your pretty little wife here will, of course, be waiting here with us. You will remove $500,000 from your bank. You will then return to your wife here. We will let you go after we get the money." Richards paused again for effect. "Rest assured, Mister Bank President, any funny stuff from you and you can kiss your pretty little wife goodbye. We will blow her fucking ass away."

Randy completed a rather mundane shift at 4 AM on Saturday. He crawled into bed with Sue by 4:30. He would be awakened by police business several hours earlier than normal.

Richards drove Bill Hamby to his home at 8:40 AM, Saturday morning. "Remember, Mister Bank President, we have your pretty little wife. If you want to see her again, you'll do as we told you to do. Also, I'll be watching."

Bill Hamby walked resolutely to the front door of his home. He turned around for one final glance at Butch Richards. His sense of foreboding was overwhelming. He continued to lament his failure to protect Mary, but he managed to pull himself together. He knew that his wife's life depended on him doing as he was told. He exited home and walked to his Lexus parked in their driveway. Richards instructed Bill Hamby to drive quietly to the bank as though it were a routine work day. Richards overlooked one key consideration: Bill Hamby did not routinely work on Saturday. His appearance at the bank would certainly be noticed!

Carol and Henry Norris lived directly across the street from the Hambys. Long time residents of Westfield, the Norris' were a congenial, outgoing couple, who were respected by their neighbors. Carol Norris was a bit of a busybody who kept up on everyone's business. She was sitting on her front porch having her third cup of coffee when Butch Richards dropped off Bill Hamby. She immediately went into newshound stance. She was certain the she had never seen the man who dropped of Bill Hamby.

Moreover, Mary Hamby was not with them. Carol Norris may have been somewhat of a busy body. Nevertheless, she was a very intelligent, observant woman. She knew that something was not right with the Hambys on this cloudy Saturday morning. She called the Westfield Police Department to report what she had seen. The desk sergeant listened patiently to Carol Norris. Most of the Westfield officers were familiar with Carol Norris. She was what cops referred to as a "frequent flier". A frequent flier to police officers is a man or woman who called the law for every little thing that occurred in their neighborhood. The desk sergeant listened patiently to Carol Norris. The hackles on the back of his neck stood up when she told the desk sergeant that Bill Hamby was President of Westfield National Bank. The desk sergeant paused for a moment prior to briefing the on-duty sergeant about Carol Norris' call. The sergeant directed the desk sergeant to immediately dispatch units to the Hamby residence and the Westfield National Bank.

Butch Richards followed Bill Hamby at a safe distance. Richards told Hamby that his wife would be shot if any cops were spotted. Hamby parked his Lexus directly even with the bank's main entrance. This in itself raised eyebrows since Bill Hamby had a reserved parking space behind the bank. Moreover, Hamby's demeanor as he entered the bank was clearly not consistent with his personality. He entered the bank's main entrance at 9:05 AM. The six bank employees present in the lobby looked up in surprise at Bill Hamby. He seldom, if ever, went to the bank on Saturday. He managed a perfunctory hello to the staff as he walked directly to his office. Bill called teller supervisor Frances Miller into his office.

Frances Miller had worked for Bill Hamby for six years. She felt that she knew him well. She could see that all was not well with Bill Hamby. He directed Frances to close his office door. Try as he may, Bill was unable to conceal why he was at the bank on a Saturday. "Frances," he said, "I don't know what to do. Mary and I were kidnapped last night. She's being held south of town. I have to take $500,000 to them. They have threatened to kill her if I don't bring the money."

Butch Richards was growing impatient. Bill Hamby had been in the Westfield National Bank for nearly ten minutes. Richards called his confederates by cell phone. "I don't know what the fuck is taking so long. If you don't hear from me in the next ten minutes, off the woman and hit road."

Bill Hamby and Frances knew that they had to do something, and they had to do it fast. What they did not know was that Carol Norris' call to the Westfield Police Department had started a sequence of events that would call on Randy and Nero to prevent the murder of an innocent Mary Hamby. The Westfield Police Department unit dispatched to the Westfield National Bank had little difficulty in identifying Butch Richards watching the bank. The Westfield officers radioed dispatch that they had a suspicious individual under observation near the bank.

Bill Hamby and Frances Miller extracted $500,000 cash from the bank vault. They placed the money, as directed by Butch Richards, in an unmarked bank bag. Bill walked through the bank lobby and out to his Lexus. He threw the bank bag into the rear seat, prior to setting off to the manufactured home. He didn't get far. Three units from the Westfield Police Department pull over Butch Richards on the Southern end of town. Richards surrendered quietly. Bill Hamby, who had witnessed the capture, turned around and frantically drove back to the scene of the take down. He identified himself, telling the police officer's that he could take them to their hideout.

15 minutes had elapsed between Butch Richards last call. They decided to take off with Carol Hamby. They decided to forgo their vehicle, surmising

that Butch Richards had been busted. They roused a terrified Mary Hamby and absconded on foot into the wooded area that defined the Southern edge of Westfield. Mary, her hands bound in front of her, had difficulty keeping up with the two thugs. Running with her hands bound in front of her was extremely difficult. That did stop her captives from forcing her to keep up with them. Mary was absolutely distraught. She did not know if her husband was alive. Moreover, she had little reason to believe that these evil men would let her go.

Bill Hamby led the Westfield Police to the abandoned manufactured home. The vehicle they had stolen, a compact sedan, was still parked in front of the home. The day shift sergeant directed officers to fan out to surround the manufactured home. With the home surrounded, the sergeant used a loud speaker to inform the thugs that they were surrounded. Ten minutes expired with no activity noted from within the home. A Westfield police officer stationed at the rear of the home contacted the shift sergeant by radio. "Hey, Sarge," he said. "You need to come around to the rear."

The entourage of police officers, led by the shift sergeant, ran around to the rear of the home, unaware of what awaited them. It was obvious that the trio had taken off towards the forest-like terrain south of Westfield. The shift sergeant did not hesitate in directing the officers to fan out. He also called dispatch, directing her to call Officer Thompson and have him report to the scene with his canine.

Sue Thompson took the call at ten minutes before 11 PM. She hated the thought of having to wake Randy. He had made it abundantly clear that he could be called at any time, day or night. He needed a few seconds to focus on waking. He had been in a deep sleep. Once focused, he sprang into action. His initial action was to call dispatch to ask what was up. Once briefed, he quickly dressed in civilian clothes. He roused Nero, who had been sleeping soundly on a large pillow in the living room of the Thompson home. The dog could sense the urgency in Randy's demeanor. Nero followed Randy to his black and white. Randy turned on his lights and drove to the address provided by dispatch.

Upon arriving at the scene, Randy was motioned to the rear of the home. The shift sergeant and several Westfield officers were waiting for Randy and Nero. "OK, Randy, looks like they ran off into the wooded area with the

Hamby woman. What can we do with the dog?" Randy provided a brief overview of tracking to the sergeant and fellow officers. He explained the fundamental considerations: human scent, climatic conditions, humidity, and terrain. Randy then explained that he would have to commence tracking right away, but would be happy to brief the various shifts in detail how a trained police dog can assist police agencies. He asked the on-site officers if they were aware of the point where the three folks entered the woods. They explained that it appeared to be at a point due south of the home.

Randy then moved Nero to the exact point where the trio had entered the woods. He then patted the ground where it appeared the two thugs and Mary Hamby entered the wooded area. The area where the track commences is called the scent pad. Randy patted the ground at the scent pad. The dog immediately began sniffing the ground. Nero locked in on the scent of the three missing persons. The big dog commenced sniffing the ground in a consistent, due south pattern. Randy closely followed Nero as the big dog followed the scent trail of the three persons. He also ran through his mind the lesson he learned from Harvey Rhodes at Southern Training Academy.

Harvey taught the class that dogs are capable of following human scent for miles and miles. Rhodes explained the difference between field scouting and tracking. Field scouting relies on human scent blown in a particular pattern through the air. Tracking, on the other hand, does not rely on airborne scent; it relies on scent particles that leave the lost person or fugitive through their clothes. Those particles are subject to gravity. The molecular components leave the quarry and cling to grass and vegetation. Those particles can cling to the grass for lengthy periods of time, easily 24 hours.

Nero remained locked in on the scent of the three. The terrain was comprised of a relatively thick grass, trees, and streams. Nero carried on, impervious to any other sounds or smells present on the track. Randy fell in line with Nero, oblivious to anything but Nero. The terrain began to dip just a bit when Nero suddenly stopped. Randy thought back again to training with Harvey. The instructor taught the class that human scent can be carried over water, in the direction the stream is flowing. That is exactly what confronted Nero and Randy.

The two fugitives had dragged Mary Hamby across the one-foot deep stream. The two thugs thought that a dog would lose the scent when it encounters water. Once again, Randy thought back to Harvey Rhodes' instruction regarding tracking and streams. Rhodes taught the class that when a lost person or fugitive crosses a stream, molecular components of their scent will be retained on the surface of the stream. Dog handlers are taught when a tracking dog encounters a stream, it is best to cross the water at a point above or below the point where the dog seemed to lose the scent.

Randy did exactly that. The stream was running north to south. The one-foot stream was running at a somewhat moderate pace. Randy decided to move to a point approximately 50 yards downstream from where Nero lost the scent. The handler/dog team forded the stream without incident. Randy continued to praise and encourage Nero, who remained deeply interested. Nero immediately regained the scent of the three people in question. The trail led due south again. Nero almost pulled Randy over in his haste to resume the track. Randy switched on his portable radio to update the police officers following closely behind. He was gratified that the Westfield Police Officers had lagged behind. He had explained that any officers preceding the tracking dog could impede the dogs' ability to follow the scent of the quarry.

Mary Hamby was absolutely exhausted when she and the two thugs happened on an abandoned shack.

They approached quietly and could quickly deduce that the shack was unoccupied. They had no idea that a contingent of police officers and one highly-trained dog were in hot pursuit. Nero was relentless in tracking the trio. The dog seemed totally consumed with the scent trail. Randy was also consumed with the situation.

The handler/dog team had tracked the missing trio for two and a half miles, when Nero hesitated prior to suddenly turning 90 degrees to the east. Randy recalled a lesson from Harvey Rhodes. The instructor had admonished his students to "trust your dog." Randy did exactly that, following Nero without hesitation. His patience was rewarded when, after another half mile, he spotted what appeared to be an abandoned hunting cabin. Randy called the shift sergeant to inform him of the cabin. The sergeant instructed Randy to stand fast with Nero until the rest of the force caught up.

Inside the abandoned cabin, the two thugs were attempting to figure out their next move. They knew in their own minds that Butch Richards must have been captured. One of thugs said, "What are we going to do now? We're screwed, man."

The other thug responded, "And what are we going to do with the woman? We sure can't take her with us. And she's seen us."

Mary Hamby was nearly apoplectic with fear. Along with her terror over her own predicament, she has no idea whether or not Bill Hamby was even alive. She could not think of any experience in her lifetime more terrifying than what was happening now. Mary Hamby was not sanguine regarding her chances for survival. Tied up and gagged, she could not even plead for her life.

Mary was unaware that she would soon be liberated. The shift sergeant asked the officers for their opinions regarding how to check the cabin. The cabin was located in a clearing, which precluded a routine approach. Randy and Nero waited behind the other police officers, anxious to contribute to the search. He couldn't wait any longer. "Sarge," he said to the shift leader, "I can take Nero around behind the cabin. The wind is blowing north to south. Nero will be able to pick up their scents if they are in there." The shift sergeant hesitated briefly before giving Randy the OK. Randy explained that he would reconnoiter around to south of the cabin, which would enable Nero to utilize his superior olfactory ability.

Randy was able to lead Nero behind the cabin without being spotted. He was proceeding cautiously; he did not want to jeopardize the Hamby woman, were they, in fact, in the cabin. Randy was pleased to discover that the clearing behind the cabin was approximately half the distance of the north side clearing. Randy calmed down Nero, who was keyed up; the big dog was aware that Randy was excited as well.

The cabin currently hiding the two thugs and Mary Hamby was well over 50 years old. It served as a base for hunters for many years. The building was constructed with wood. Little had been done over the years to address the upkeep of the cabin. Years of neglect had rendered the building very porous. The scent of the three persons holed up in the old cabin was escaping the cabin. Randy could sense that Nero had already hit on the scent. He pulled out his portable radio, ensuring that the volume was low enough to not tip off the two thugs. Randy called the shift sergeant to inform him that Nero was showing interest in the cabin. That's were it all went bad.

The shift sergeant instructed Randy to use discretion regarding searching the cabin. Randy whispered to Nero, "Find him, boy." The suspicious command instantly raised Nero's interest. Randy followed Nero as the big dog, in a slow, meticulous pattern, worked his way directly to the south end of the cabin. Randy remained on high alert, his adrenaline rising off the charts. He was certain Mary Hamby and the two perpetrators were in the cabin. Moreover, he felt that the two thugs would be watching the north side of the cabin, where he felt they would be looking for the police.

Westfield Police Officer David Henderson had been on the force for 12 years. He was known for his quick temper and disdain for authority. He has been reprimanded too many times to count. Henderson was one of the contingent of officers standing by for instructions. In his mind, he felt that the shift sergeant was a weak individual who was hesitant when faced with a stressful incident. Henderson then began to drift away from the assembled officers. He moved silently to the right, or west of the assembled officers. The rogue cop felt that he could boost his image with Chief Benson if he rescued the woman. Arresting the two perps would serve as icing on the cake.

Henderson continued circling to the west side of the cabin. The contingent of offices on scene were too occupied to notice Henderson's departure. Randy could not see Henderson. Nero could not see Henderson either; but he could hear him. People have long been aware of the phenomenal olfactory ability of dogs. Estimates range from 100 times that of a human being. Most folks believe it is far more substantial than that. Harvey Rhodes' lesson to Randy and the class was this: dogs can smell intruders or lost persons for vast distances. Moreover, they can hear much better than humans. They can pick up very slight noises at substantial distances. David Henderson's desire to seek glory by freeing the Hamby woman was about to detonate. Henderson stepped on some twigs as he endeavored to sneak up on the cabin. He grimaced, certain that the noise made by the twigs gave away his position. He froze in place, until he was certain he had not given away his position.

The tension inside the cabin was palpable. The thugs were becoming more paranoid by the minute. Mary Hamby's nerves were at the breaking point. Each additional moment amplified her belief that the situation was hopeless. She regretted that she had not told her husband that she loved him enough. She regretted that she and her husband had not been able to have a child. She remained curled up in the fetal position, still tied up and gagged.

The situation imploded in a series of calamities no one could have dreamed up on their own. The shift sergeant, unaware of Henderson's maverick move, ordered the contingent of officers to commence a methodical advancement towards the cabin. The two thugs lifted Mary Hamby to her feet as they prepared to leave the cabin. One of the thugs glanced out of a window and saw several Westfield Police Officers moving towards the cabin. "Lets get the fuck out of here. The place is crawling with cops."

Randy Thompson, sensing that something was happening, unsnapped Nero from his leash. Handlers are taught that the split second it takes to unleash their dog could be the difference between someone escaping or being seriously injured. Moreover, Harvey Rhodes emphasized that a well-trained dog can be controlled by the handler, regardless of the situation.

With Westfield Police Officers closing in from the north, David Henderson, not wanting to miss the opportunity for glory, advanced from the east side of the cabin. Finally, Randy emerged from the south, on full alert, with Nero keyed up; the big dog easily picked up his handler's eagerness. With the stage set, the situation detonated.

As the two thugs exited the cabin from the back door, or the south side of the cabin, the cops arrived at the front, or north side of the cabin. David Henderson, operating in his rogue manner, arrived near the cabin at the southeast corner as the three people exited the cabin. The two shoved Mary Hamby, still tied up, out on to the ground behind the cabin as Henderson prepared to charge into the cabin like Superman saving the day! Randy, taking it all in, had to struggle to hold onto Nero, who was off-leash. Henderson, with thoughts of heroism dancing in his head, almost fainted when he came face to face with the two thugs and Mary Hamby.

The thugs panicked and split up, one running south and one east. Randy saw what was going down and reacted. The thug who had initially run west surrendered to the Westfield Officers approaching from the west. The other thug, who had nearly collided with a startled Henderson, lit out to the east. Randy Thompson saw that Westfield Officers were securing Mary Hamby, ordered the perpetrator running east to HALT! The individual ignored Randy's command. Randy again challenged the individual, who once again ignored him.

A German Shepherd can run at a top speed of 38 miles per hour. The human being who can outrun a Shepherd has not been born. Randy, satisfied that he had clearly challenged the individual, released Nero with an enthusiastic, "Get him, boy." The perpetrator ran at full stride, approximately 75 yards from where Randy had commanded the big dog to attack. The big dog would require just a few seconds to reach the fleeing thug. Nero would not effect a take down! As Nero closed on the fleeing thug, Westfield Police Officer David Henderson, feeling that he could overtake the individual, stepped into the bead that Nero was on towards the fleeing thug.

Police dogs can begin to recognize police officers. Television programs like COPS show instances where a police dog is clearly able to differentiate between perps and police. They can be seen barking at the suspect only. David Henderson would not have that result. With Nero in full stride, the rogue police officer stepped directly in front of the charging dog.

Nero did not have sufficient time to distinguish the police officer from the fleeing thug. The charging German Shepherd collided with Henderson as the officer ran after the criminal. Taken by surprise, Nero responded in a manner consistent with his training. Nero lunged at Henderson, hitting him chest high. Randy and the Westfield Police Officers stared in horror as Henderson endeavored to ward off the frenzied dog. Randy arrived within seconds. He immediately pulled Nero off Henderson. The police officer had suffered significant bites and puncture wounds. Several officers chased down the second thug.

Randy had secured Nero and moved him away from the chaotic scene. Henderson was screaming at Randy and Nero. "What the fuck are you doing, sic-ing that fucking dog on me?" Randy was standing about 25 yards from Henderson, the shift sergeant, and the rest of the Westfield Police Officers. Henderson was taken to a police cruiser for transport to Westfield General Hospital. His injuries were not life-threatening. Henderson would be laid up for a period of time.

The shift sergeant approached Randy and Nero. He was unaware of Henderson's rogue behavior. "Randy, what the hell happened? This doesn't look good. Henderson is seriously injured."

Randy, very subdued, said, "I don't know, Sarge. Nero had a bead on the guy when Henderson jumped out from behind the cabin before I could react."

The sergeant replied with a question. “Did you say that Henderson jumped out from behind the cabin?”

When Randy affirmed that Henderson had indeed acted on his own, the shift sergeant rolled his eyes. “Don’t worry, Randy. I think I know what happened. Write up a statement for me before the shift ends.”

Chapter 9

The fallout from the Henderson incident shot through Westfield like a cannonball. Randy briefed Mayor Johnson and Chief Benson. The mayor seemed far more concerned than Chief Benson. "Don't worry about this, Randy. We've spoken to Henderson. He fessed up to trying to take down those two and save the Hamby woman on his own. He'll be laid up for a while. Let's prepare a protocol for instruction for all shifts. We have to do whatever it takes to prevent this type of incident." Randy thanked the chief for his support.

The rank and file officers were split about fifty-fifty on the incident. They were very much aware of that Henderson was responsible for his injuries. He would be none the worse for wear in a month or so. Nevertheless, Henderson had friends who were not pleased with what happened.

The Henderson incident, occurring so soon after Randy and Nero went to work, exposed an attitude felt by numerous nascent handlers. Police officers, like most working people, love their jobs. It is a high stress, strenuous occupation. Police officers resent any circumstance that may cut into their opportunity for career advancement. Many police officers see canines as detriments to their careers. Westfield was not exempt from that situation. Their attitudes were not ameliorated by the headline on the front page of the next day's Westfield Times: WESTFIELD BANK PRESIDENT & WIFE RESCUED FOLLOWING KIDNAPPING. The sub headlines highlighted how the entire incident went down. The text also explained Nero's involvement, including the injury to Henderson.

The crime wave sweeping Westfield continued to grow. One of it's architects laughed out loud after reading the Westfield Times story about the previous days' incident. Ernie Olsen, a 26-year-old white male, had moved to Westfield from Oakland, California six months prior. Olsen had escaped Oakland in response to the police war on gangs and gang related violence. Born and raised on the mean streets of Oakland, Olsen had to learn to take care of himself at a very early age. Moreover, Olsen's father had left him and his mother when he was four years old. Being raised by a single parent with no support from his father left he and his mother destitute. Try as she may, his mother could barely keep a roof over Ernie's head and food in his belly.

Ernie's deprivation from a young age fueled a burning desire to improve his and his mother's life. Ernie loved and respected his mother. Sans siblings, Ernie had only his mother to care him. Ernie had unconditional love for his mother. He hated his father.

Ernie seldom had new clothes. He frequently wore tattered clothing and shoes. A burning desire had festered inside of Ernie. As he entered his teen years, he became more and more hardened. He was arrested five times before his 14th birthday. Charges against him ranged from petty theft to possession of marijuana with intent to distribute. Several stints in juvenile detention had little effect.

Ernie Olsen was completely out of control by his 17th birthday. His mother had basically given up on him. She was told by neighborhood youths that Ernie had joined a gang. That gang was the Bloods. The Bloods were the putative kings of the Bay Area. Ernie worked his way up the food chain by collecting drug money from clients with tardy payment habits. The word on the mean streets of Oakland was that you had better pay before Ernie Olsen paid you a visit. Ernie never made it into the upper level of the Oakland chapter of the Bloods. Word on the streets was that Ernie had whacked a handful of the "clients" who were consistently late with their debts.

The reputation he had developed as a strongman for the Bloods was bringing far too much heat from the cops. Ernie was "invited" to hit the road. Conventional wisdom regarding gangs was that you were a "lifer", which meant exactly that. You were not permitted to leave. Gang members understood that it was for life. Members like Ernie were permitted to leave in good standing. The notorious gangs like the Bloods and Crips wanted to expand their empire towards the east. The Blood leadership directed Ernie Olsen to set up shop in Westfield. He would do so with a vengeance.

Randy and Nero were back on the job. The public and city government were supportive of Randy Thompson's action. The same could not be said for a number of rank and file Westfield police officers. Randy saw his first episode of harassment from fellow officers a few days following the Henderson incident. Upon arriving for duty with Nero, Randy found a replica of a giant dog biscuit taped to his locker. As he opened his locker, the public-address system began a series of dog barking and dog's gags that brought smiles to everyone in the building. Despite the fact some mild animosity/jealously existed, most officers were very accepting of the handler/dog team.

Assimilating Nero into his routine patrolling regimen was a process that would take time. A police dog handler must accomplish his or her duties with a number of considerable concerns. Harvey Rhodes was very exacting during his introduction to aggression training. Harvey spoke to the class in a very deliberate manner. "It is imperative that you understand that your partner on the end of the leash is a weapon. The responsibility for safety is clearly on the handler." Harvey paused for effect. "It's the same as the weapon we carry. Just as we are responsible for our sidearms, you are responsible for your dog. You can imagine the heat we would receive for firing our weapons in an unauthorized manner. The same applies to police dogs." Randy and his classmates could see how passionate their instructor was regarding this topic. Harvey concluded that instruction; he clearly had their undivided attention as he told the class, "Men, you can have been 99 successful actions with your dog. If episode 100 results in an innocent person being bitten, well, I think you get the message."

Ernie Olsen wasted little time in getting his operation going. He learned quickly that Westfield's gangs were not up to the "standards" of an organization like the Bloods, Crips, or Banditos. Olsen snooped around Westfield for a few days following his arrival in town. He immediately saw that Westfield was a potential gold mine. It took only a couple of days for Ernie Olsen to realize that Westfield was ripe for pillaging. It was clearly understood that the Blood's national organization, once established, demanded that local chapters abide by the California standards. The local leader was responsible to the "headquarters," located in Oakland, California. The existing gang members quickly fell in line with Ernie Olsen. He quickly established a hierarchy for the Westfield chapter. The putative leader prior to Olsen's arrival, Butch Carter, immediately fell in lock step with Ernie Olsen.

Randy was on routine patrol with Nero on a quiet Saturday night. The time was 11 PM. Ernie Olson, now firmly entrenched as the hood's boss in Westfield, had directed Butch Carter to ramp up activities in and around Westfield. Carter and four other Bloods were set to hit Martel's Supermarket after it closed its doors at 11 PM. Martel's was one of the primary supermarkets in Westfield. Ernie Olsen speculated that Martel's would easily have $3,000 to $4,000 cash on hand at closing time. The plan, as laid out by Olsen to Carter, was for four Bloods to enter Martel's just prior to closing time. While casing Martel's, Olsen had observed that the Martel's staff was very patient with late-arriving customers. This, he reasoned, would be an easy mark for the gang.

Randy had stopped at a city park to allow Nero to hike his leg. He sat himself down on a picnic table. Nero finished his business and returned directly to his partner. Randy sat there with Nero enjoying a very pleasant evening when his portable radio crackled with an urgent message for all units: "Attention all units, a 211 in process, Martel's Supermarket."

Randy sprang into action. "Come on, boy," he said to Nero. The big dog instantly headed for Randy's cruiser. It wasn't necessary for Randy to say anything else to Nero, for the dog to understand that this incident was real.

A gigantic argument has raged for decades regarding whether or not dogs can think. Randy, en route to Martel's, flashed back in his mind to training with Harvey Rhodes. Harvey said to the class during field scouting. "Let me tell you all something you'll encounter with your dogs when you're back in your respective cities. Any of you rookie dog handlers have any idea of what I'm talking about?" He paused to allow his students think about the question. After waiting for a few more seconds Harvey said to his students, "It's simple: the argument about whether or not dogs can think." Randy Thompson and his classmates were instantly mesmerized. All of them, like most Americans, were of the opinion that dogs can definitely think. A classmate of Randy's boldly proclaimed, "I am certain that dogs can think. How can they possibly do all the things they do without the ability think?"

Harvey was ready for that question. He could not count the number of times he had responded to a person convinced that dogs think. Harvey responded to that question exactly as he had for years. "The answer to that question is simple. No one has been able successfully prove that dogs think. Moreover, we have all seen dogs do things that seemingly would require thought." Harvey paused for effect, "What we do know is that dogs may or may not possess the ability to think. We do know they can remember." Harvey then asked the class if anyone had seen a TV report showing a United States service man or women returning home after a one-year deployment. What routinely happens is that the dog seems to hesitate for a second or two, then absolutely attacks the person returning in a frenzy of hugging and licking. He concluded that particular lesson by reiterating, "They may or may not be capable of thought. They can, however, remember!"

Butch Carter and four other Bloods had entered Martel's at 10:55. The five Bloods were wearing political masks - Richard Nixon, George W. Bush, etc. Carter ordered the manager, who had been standing near the entrance ready to lock up, to immediately lock the doors. Carter then ordered to manager to take them to the office where the store safe was located.

The nervous manager, who was entirely rattled, needed several tries to unlock the safe. When his second attempt failed, he received a slap to his face by Carter. "Listen," he told the rattled manager, "one more screw up, it will be your last." The safe opened, Carter ordered the manager to fill a bank bag with all of the paper money. The manager complied, quickly filling the bag despite shaking violently. Carter then ordered the remaining employees into the manager's office. He admonished the manager and employees to wait for five minutes before emerging from the office. Carter then ripped the phone from the wall. Finally, he ordered all of the employees to hand over their cell phones. Butch Carter put the cell phones in the bag with the cash.

A Martel's employee, Frank Collins, had managed to hide behind one of the meat counters. He was a 21-year-old college student who worked several evenings per week, as well as weekends. His family could not provide him with the funds for tuition, books, or housing. Frank still resided with his folks; he wanted to complete his studies at community college. Frank was persuing a degree in mathematics. He had been raised by Samuel and Rose Collins. The Collins had instilled a strong work ethic in Frank and his two younger sisters. It was that work ethic and responsibility that turned Westfield upside down on this pleasant evening.

Butch Carter, pleased with how easy the heist had gone over, ordered the gang of five out of Martel's via the loading dock. Frank Collins, unaware of how his fellow employees had fared, decided that he had to do something. He crawled out from behind the meat counter, moving on his hands and knees to a checkout line where he hit a panic button. The panic button sounded at the precise moment the gang of Bloods exited the manager's office. Carter heard the panic button sounding as he and the gang reached the loading dock. He realized that the panic button would also send an alert to the Westfield Police Department.

Frank Collins, his adrenaline going through the roof, decided to creep in the direction of the manager's office. He felt that he could not look at himself in a mirror if he did not try to save them. After low-crawling along aisle two to the rear of Martel's, Collins hesitated, unsure of what to do next. That decision was taken away when two of the Bloods noticed Collins hiding behind a stand full of apples. The two Bloods yelled out to Carter that they had spotted by an employee next to the island of apples. It wouldn't have mattered except for one minor fact: one of the Bloods had removed his mask *before* the gang members had exited Martel's. Butch Carter freaked out, shoving one of the brainless Bloods on his way to Frank Collins' hiding place. Carter, enraged by the stupidity of two of his confederates, ran to the terrorized young man.

Frank Collins appeared to understand that his life was about to end. Carter grabbed Collins and dragged him into the small corridor leading to the managers' office. The enraged Blood cronie screamed at the two idiots who had exposed their faces to Frank Collins. "You stupid sons of bitches! You gave yourselves away, you two get rid of him!" One of the two bumbling idiots drew a Glock 9 from his belt. He shot Frank Collins between the eyes without hesitation. The group of five Bloods quickly exited Martel's via the loading dock. The entire episode took exactly nine minutes. The terrorized manager and employees remained frozen in place.

The first Westfield Police Department Officers arrived at Martel's by 11:10 PM. None of the employees or Bloods were in view. The five Bloods had escaped in a pickup truck they had stolen earlier in the evening. The manager and employees emerged, almost tripping over Frank Collins' body. The manager ran to the front of the store to allow the Westfield Police Officers into the store, guns drawn. The police must first protect themselves when entering a potentially hostile situation. The manager was quickly able to convince the responding officers that he was indeed the manager of Martel's.

The responding officers, guns drawn, worked their way throughout the supermarket until they were able to declare it cleared. The body of Frank Collins lay in the hallway leading to the manager's office. The Westfield Police Officers were not accustomed to such gruesome scenes. Collins has been shot between his eyes. There was no doubt that he was dead. The shift sergeant gathered himself and took command of the situation. Officers were assigned duties commonly found at homicide site. The shift sergeant entered the manager's office; it looked as though the staff sitting on chairs and the floor were traumatized by what had transpired. The shift sergeant interviewed the manager. The manager provided a coherent sequence of events. He indicated that he and the remaining staff did not witness the execution of Frank Collins. Collins was described as a hard-working, respectful young man. The manager then mused, "He was just a great young man. He died trying to get to us, to help us. He was very close to his family. I don't know how they will be able to handle this incident."

Randy Thompson and Nero arrived at Martel's within five minutes of the initial radio call. He could see that several black and white units were already on scene. He remained in stand-by status just outside the main entrance. Randy was shocked to see an EMS unit pull up to the entrance of Martel's and hustle inside, pushing a stretcher ahead of them. Little did Randy know that the EMS folks were there to recover a body – Frank Collins!

Chapter 10

Butch Carter and the Bloods had piled into the vehicle they had stolen prior to hitting Martel's. Carter was still furious over the blunder two of the Bloods had made.

"Olsen is going to be furious with you two idiots. How could you two been so fucking stupid?"

Carter's cell phone rang, as he completed his excoriation of the two. Ernie Olsen called, wanting a report on how things went down at Martel's. Carter related the story, to include the two nitwits who had removed their masks, making killing the employee necessary.

Ernie Olsen blew a gasket! He unloaded on Butch Carter for several minutes. "What the fuck were those idiots thinking? Listen Butch, drop those sons of bitches off and tell them to lay low for a couple of days. I'll deal with them in a day or two." Carter pulled over about ten miles south of Westfield. He turned to the two Bloods riding behind him. "Listen, you two, the boss told me to drop you off. He wants you to lay low until this thing blows over." The two Bloods looked crestfallen. But they knew that they would have to comply. They thought better of protesting.

Randy Thompson felt a palpable disappointment at not being involved in the initial response. He realized that incidents were going to occur wherein the use of a police dog would not be practical. He also realized that a police dog can be an invaluable asset away from the scene. Harvey Rhodes had related several examples of how dogs were able to track fugitives who had been able to escape from the scene of the crime.

"Listen up, guys," Harvey said, "an Air Force dog handler from the Department of Defense assisted civilian police in tracking down a fugitive who had robbed a platoon of airman. The individual had dressed in Air Force clothing. The Air Force dog handler tracked down the culprit a few miles from the air base. The individual, armed with a Smith-Wesson revolver, surrendered meekly." Harvey advised the new handlers that it may take time for the rank and file to accept the specific abilities a dog brings to the program. Randy knew that assimilation may take time. His status would change for the better by the time this night was over.

Butch Carter continued to seethe as the Bloods traveled south of Westfield. He knew that Ernie Olsen had exploded when he learned of the debacle in Westfield. Carter pulled the stolen van into a rest stop. He wanted to lay low until he determined whether or not the cops were following. Butch let an hour pass by without any signs of the law.

The Westfield Police surmised that the gang had headed out of town to the south. The state police had been notified. Randy Thompson remained in the background as the investigation unraveled what had transpired. He was hesitant to interrupt the shift sergeant to ask if he could help. He really lit up when an officer hurriedly ran up to the shift sergeant. "Sarge," said the heavy officer, "it looks as though they had a vehicle behind Martel's. It appears that they went south." Randy, standing by looking bored, determined that this may be his opportunity.

Randy waited for an opportunity to ask the shift sergeant for permission to utilize Nero to search for the Bloods. The shift sergeant seemed annoyed at the interruption. "Go ahead, Thompson. Keep me posted." Randy thanked the sergeant and doubled-timed back to his black and white. He loaded Nero into his cruiser and headed south. He knew that he had a slight chance of success. Nonetheless, he was determined to find the gang.

Randy headed south with Nero in a state anticipation. Once again the big dog knew that something was up. Randy's mind was running at a mile a minute. He reminded himself that the people on the loose had murdered a young man for no apparent reason. Heading south, Randy endeavored to put himself in the position of the killers. He thought that they would avoid the obvious places. What he could not answer was whether or not the gang had split up or remained together. The gang had gotten away without anyone seeing their vehicle.

The handler/dog team continued south, with Randy losing confidence. He observed a rest stop ahead and thought it would be worth a look. Moreover, Nero could use a break to hike his leg. Randy observed several civilians relaxing at the rest area. The small group perked up when they saw Nero. "Good evening, folks," he said, as Nero trotted off into the woods. One of the women in the group asked Randy the standard questions about Nero. After telling the group about police dogs, he explained why he was on the road with Nero. A gentleman spoke up immediately. "Officer," he said, "we saw a group of five men in a van. They were arguing amongst themselves. They then split up. Three rode off in the van." Randy lit up immediately. He asked the gentleman what had happened to the other two. The gentleman pointed to the wooded area, stating that they went that way.

Randy immediately radioed the information to headquarters. He gave them the mile marker. The folks were asked to stay and brief the responding officers. Randy snapped his leash to Nero's chain. He once again thanked the folks for their assistance. He led Nero to an opening in the trees and enthusiastically commanded the big dog to track. Nero immediately went into working mode. The big dog dipped his nose to the ground. Tracking these two criminals would be a snap for Nero. The fleeing fugitives were, of course, sweating heavily. Their scent was heavy; it clung to the vegetation. Randy was pleased. Conditions could not have been better.

The two thugs had traveled several miles into the forest. They felt that they traveled far enough off of the highway to allow them to rest. Bad choice. Nero tracked the two with little difficulty. He encountered few obstacles. The big dog quickly closed the gap between the fugitives who, after a brief rest, continued on away from highway. They had little concern regarding the possibility of being caught.

Nero tracked the two Bloods with unrelenting determination. The dog handler was trained to let the dog work the trail of the quarry. The perfect tracking trial or real search occurs when the dog hears the word "track" one time. Should the dog hesitate or lose interest, the handler will endeavor to regenerate the track by making a small circle or figure eight. Nero did not require reinforcement. He searched without hesitation. That dogged determination would result in another example of a dog's olfactory capability.

Dog handlers endeavor to minimize noise during tracking situations. Adhesive tape on the choke collar minimizes noise. There is, however, one element that cannot be controlled: a dog's panting. A panting dog, when tracking, can be heard from long distances. Background noises like automobiles and airplanes distract the tracking dog. This search, however, was in a rural, bucolic terrain. Randy had indeed covered the choke collar. He could not, however, control Nero's panting. Veterinarians and animal psychologists have taught dog handlers how critical panting is to a dog. Like humans, dogs breathe in accelerated numbers when they exert themselves. Tracking is usually the longest running trial presented to a police dog. Naturally, the longer the track, the louder the panting.

The two fugitives heard Nero panting as he closed the gap. They immediately lit out in the same direction they had moved since being dumped by Butch Carter. They realized that they were not going to succeed in shaking off the dog and handler.

They then came up with what they thought was a solution to their dilemma. After crossing a small creek, they decided to confuse the dog by climbing two oak trees. They thought that the dog would lose their scent if they climbed a tree. What they didn't know is that human scent is subject to gravity. The scent of a person hiding in a tree will fall to the ground. A mild breeze will disperse the scent in a wider but weaker scent cone. A stiff breeze will cause the scent cone to flow away from the source a narrower, but stronger concentration.

Nero continued to track the duo. He and Randy had closed the gap separating them from the two thugs. They had closed to within 100 yards of their quarry. Nero's relentless pursuit had begun to take its toll. Randy pulled up and reigned in Nero to allow the dog to rest and take some water. Randy had to assure Nero that everything was under control. The big dog lapped up water from Randy's canteen for a few seconds, then began to growl in a low, suspicious manner. Randy was on his feet in a split second. Nero had responded to the scent of the duo. A prevailing southerly wind had suddenly shifted to the west. It took just a moment or two for the scent of the thugs to hit Nero squarely in his nose.

Randy knew that the duo was very close. Harvey Rhodes had explained to his class that a dog handler should be able to recognize the various responses from their dogs to different stimulus. "For example," said Harvey, "your dogs will respond one way to the scent of humans and in a different manner for an animal. Most dogs will respond in a stealthy manner to humans, and another manner for animals. Each dog is different. You have to study your own dogs' mannerisms. It could save your life."

Nero demonstrated a calm, stealthy approach. Randy immediately recognized that Nero was working the scent with his nose raised. That was Randy's signal to look ahead, versus tracking the quarry. The wind shift had presented Nero with a slam dunk. The scent of the two thugs traveled just a few yards before Nero responded by barking and trying to climb the tree currently inhabited by two very startled thugs. Randy commanded the duo to climb down, one at a time, hands up. The first individual complied with Randy's command. The excited Westfield officer ordered the second thug to do likewise. The second culprit followed the first. Nero was on high alert. The duo was terrified by Nero's presence.

Randy could hear the Westfield contingent approaching. His attention, however, was concentrated on the two individuals before him. He had to search them to ensure that they weren't armed. The method utilized by dog handlers is to have the perp stand approximately 10 to 12 feet away from the dog. They are instructed to raise their hands and spread their legs. The dog handler then utters the standard phrase: "I have a trained police dog. He is trained to attack on my command. He is also trained to attack without command should you resist or present any hostile move. Do you understand what I have told you?" The two thugs indicated that they did understand. Randy proceeded to search the first individual. Nero's attention was riveted on the other individual.

Randy completed searching the first thug without finding a weapon. He reinforced the warning that Nero would attack if provoked. He carefully transitioned to the second thug. Nero remained completely focused on the two individuals. The Westfield Police contingent was just a few yards when it happened. Randy was in the middle of searching the second individual when he discovered the .357 revolver in his belt.

With Randy's attention centered on the weapon, and the Westfield Police entering the clearing, the first individual thought that the time was right for a second opportunity at freedom. German Shepherds can run 38 miles per hour. They are nowhere near the speed of a Greyhound. They are, however, much faster than any human. This genius had not covered 20 yards when Nero took him down. The big dog had snagged the thug's left arm. The terrorized thug gave give up, screaming to Randy to get the dog off him.

The shift sergeant and fellow officers stood there, totally dumbfounded by Nero's performance. Nero had once again validated a very critical element of police dogs. A truly fundamental principle of police dog training is this: minimal force only is used to subdue or apprehend an offender. Nero used the minimal force required to subdue the individual. Police dog instructors have consistently preached to dog handlers that dogs are not used to inflict punishment or pain on offenders. To be sure, incidents have occurred where excessive force was used. A police dog is a legal weapon.

Randy Thompson could not describe how proud he was. Nero clearly validated the canine program. The shift sergeant walked up to Randy, who had secured Nero and was giving the dog a drink of water. "Randy," he said, "I don't know what to say. That dog is fantastic."

Randy responded in a modest tone, "Thank you, Sergeant. I am very proud of my dog."

The sergeant, obviously sincere, told Randy, "Head on back to headquarters and file your report. Great job!"

Chapter 11

Ernie Olsen was livid upon hearing of the events that had transpired following the Martel's fiasco. He railed at Butch Carter, "What the fuck were they thinking? Damn it, Butch, you were supposed to run the show. If they're caught, we're screwed! How do we know that they won't sing like birds if they are caught? They could lead the cops right here!" We're going to have to lay low." Ernie was somewhat placated when Butch Carter handed over $2,200 cash from the Martel's job. Ernie then stunned the three Bloods when he told them the two might have to be eliminated. "Right now," he said, "we have to lay low. I'll call you when things die down." Ernie gave the three a cut of the loot. He also admonished them to not flash the money around town.

Randy and Nero received a hero's welcome at headquarters. Lt. Dawson, seldom seen or heard, took this opportunity to glad hand Randy and the shift sergeant. Dawson briefed Chief Benson by phone. The chief thanked Dawson and asked him to pass along his congratulations to Randy. Randy could not have wished for a better beginning to Nero's impact in Westfield. Nero had, in the first month of duty, rescued a bank president and apprehended two of five Bloods following a robbery at Martel's supermarket.

Randy's attitude and outlook could not have been any better. Most of the rank and file officers had now accepted the handler/dog team. Randy had taken to heart the advice Harvey Rhodes had imparted regarding grabbing headlines. Randy made it his practice to praise Nero and his fellow officers.

Harvey related to Randy's class several examples wherein police dog handlers had made it their practice to take credit each time they were involved in an incident. Harvey Rhodes had stressed to his students the critical need for dog handlers to ingratiate themselves with rank and file officers. "Some officers" Harvey said to the class, "feel somewhat put off that canine handlers can gain notoriety in short order. Many officers can go through a significant portion of their careen without any high-profile case. Make sure that you assimilate Nero as though he were another officer."

Ernie Olsen was not a man who rested on his laurels. He knew that the two idiots incarcerated in the Westfield jail wouldn't hesitate to rat out him and his subordinates. Ernie decided that something had to be done, and fast. He decided that one way to protect himself was ensure that the two should be wacked. But how to do it? He called Butch Carter and set up a meeting just south of town. Ernie theorized that the Westfield Police had not made for him or Butch. That advantage would enable them to reconnoiter the Westfield Police headquarters. Butch looked at Olsen as though the boss man had bumped his head. Olsen then told Carter that he had a plan. The thug, his interest piqued, listened as Ben laid out what they had to do.

Butch Carter knew that Ernie Olsen was dead serious. He had learned from the start that Ernie seldom hesitated when he set his mind to something. "Hey, boss," Butch asked, "how are we going to pull that off?" Ernie glared at Butch while saying, "Let me worry about that. Let's hit the road back to that hick town and take care of those idiots before we're in there with them."

The shift sergeant and his subordinates wasted little time in processing the two thugs that had been captured by Randy and Nero. The two thugs refused adamantly to give up any information regarding the Bloods. Following processing, the Bloods were placed in the Westfield Police Department Jail. Like many jails around the country, the Westfield Jail was not designed for long term incarceration. They would be arraigned the following morning.

Randy and Nero were completing their busy shift at 3:45 AM. Randy was anxious to get home to Susan and fill her in on the Martel's caper. With the paperwork complete, Randy said goodbye to the cops in the office, gathered Nero and his equipment, and headed for the parking lot behind headquarters. Nero, who sat quietly at Randy's feet, needed a break.

Ernie Olsen had learned to be prepared for anything. That preparation included explosives. Butch Carter nearly fell over when Ernie told him that they were going to blow the two Bloods currently in the Westfield Jail. Ernie told Butch that they were going to blow up the jail. "That's right" Ernie told Butch, "we're going to blast those two to pieces." The two leaders of the Bloods, Westfield faction, headed for town. In the trunk of Olsen's car, safely packaged, were three sticks of commercial dynamite.

Olsen and Carter arrived at the Westfield Police headquarters where the jail was located at 3 AM. They parked two blocks from police headquarters. Olsen and Carter cased the police center and quickly discovered that the jail was located at the rear of the facility, at ground level. There were four cells, which allowed direct access. They simply had to listen in order to determine which cell the two idiot Bloods were in. Olsen and Carter made their back to Ernie's car where they retrieved the dynamite. They made their way back to the jail.

Commercial dynamite is very fragile. Persons utilizing dynamite must understand the sensitive nature of this particular explosive. Commercial dynamite is nitroglycerin-based. Olsen had learned to work with dynamite in California as a young man. Ernie had worked in a quarry prior to discovering that working for a living required effort. He had acquired some of the sensitive explosives from a local construction company. He explained to Butch Carter the process for detonating dynamite. Ernie also explained the intrinsic danger involved in using commercial dynamite.

The two Bloods incarcerated in cell # 4 had no idea of what was to befall them. The confluence of the two Bloods, Ernie Olsen and Butch Carter, and Randy Thompson and Nero occurred at 3:50 AM. The two Bloods were brooding over their situation; Olsen and Carter low-crawled to the cell block, as Randy cut Nero loose to hike his leg. Olsen and Carter looked once again to ensure that the coast was clear. Satisfied, they moved stealthily to the rear of the Westfield Police headquarters. They were able to easily determine which cell the two idiots were in, as they carried on a running conversation about their situation. Olsen and Carter had to hold back laughter as they planted the explosive at the base of the building. Olsen had installed a timing device, set for two minutes, sufficient time for them to high tail it back to Olsen's car.

"Come on, boy, let's head on home." Nero was programmed to understand and anticipate directions from Randy. Satisfied with his night's work, and anxious to fill in Susan on the Martel's incident. Randy would not be able to ride home with Nero for a number of hours. Nero finished his business and happily ran back to his partner when it happened. The big German Shepherd rounded the police complex and was making a bee line to his master when the explosives detonated.

The explosion leveled the four cells at the rear of the Westfield Police Center. The two incarcerated Bloods died instantly. Three other, less notorious inmates were severely injured, one critically. Nero was saved from serious injury, as he was shielded by a large oak tree. Randy was sufficiently far enough away from the facility to avoid real harm. He received a number of cuts and abrasions, none serious. Randy's immediate concern was Nero. The German Shepherd did not sustain any injuries, save for a few minor cuts.

Although Nero did not suffer physical injuries, the psychological effect would haunt him for a brief period of time. Alpha dogs, even a particularly strong dog like Nero, can be affected by sudden, unexpected calamities like explosions. Military and police dogs are acclimated to gunfire and explosions in a training exercise by having an individual firing blanks at a reasonable distance. The distance between the dog and blank fire is gradually decreased until the dog basically ignores the report. The same principles apply to explosives. Acclimating dogs to explosives is essentially the same as gunfire. The desired result is for the dog to have no reaction to gunfire or explosives. A dog that barks at gunfire or explosives jeopardizes the safety of the dog handler.

The explosion rocked Randy Thompson. It took him a few seconds to regain bearings following the explosion. His immediate concern was to locate Nero to ensure that his partner was OK. Nero was stunned, but not seriously injured. A phalanx of Westfield Police officers, stunned but uninjured, made their way to the jail cells. Fortunately, none of the Westfield officers were in the cell area when the dynamite exploded. The two Bloods weren't so fortunate. Both died instantly.

Randy ran to Nero, his heart beating. Nero looked at him, bewilderingly unaware of what had transpired. Randy was relieved to see that Nero had not suffered any apparent injuries. The shift sergeant and a number of officers, unaware that Randy and Nero were close to the explosion, made a quick survey of the jail area. They were gratified to spot the handler/team, both alive and uninjured. Several officers checked on Randy and Nero while the shift sergeant and other officers checked the demolished jail cells. They quickly ascertained that both of the incarcerated Bloods did not survive the blast.

A reluctant Randy Thompson was taken to Westfield General Hospital. He was more concerned with Nero's condition. Randy drove post haste to the vet's office when he was released from the hospital. He was emotional when the vet finished with the dog. The vet told Randy that Nero would be fine. "Thanks, Doc," Randy said to the vet. "I don't know what I would do if I lost Nero." The vet advised Randy to let Nero rest for a day or two.

The scene at the jail was chaotic. The police officers did not know if the explosion was isolated, or part of a larger conspiracy. A check of the jail did not uncover any additional explosives or problems. The jail cells were destroyed. The remains of the two Bloods were found buried in the rubble that was the jail. Chief Benson was called. He dressed and made his way to the police complex. The shift sergeant briefed the chief. The mayor inquired in to the condition of Randy Thompson and Nero.

Randy was not able to shed any light on the deceased Bloods. Chief Benson asked Randy if there was anything that he could say about to two deceased individuals. "I'm sorry, Chief," said Randy. "I did not see anything that would point us in the direction of what happened. But let me tell you, it seems like quite a coincidence, doesn't it?"

Randy's wife Sue, who had been called to the hospital, took Randy and Nero home. Randy was, as expected, very wired up following the near-death experience. Nero was also jittery. The big dog would be fine, although it would take a few days.

Chapter 12

Ernie Olsen and Butch made it safely to the motel they had been occupying since arriving in Westfield. They shared a good laugh over the incident. "I'll bet you those two idiots didn't know what hit them," Carter said to Ernie.

"You're right, Butch," replied Ernie, "but we'd better hope those stupid sons of bitches didn't narc us out. We're going to have to lay low for while. I'll feel better when we can confirm that they're dead."

Randy took off for the next two days. He and Susan concentrated solely on rebuilding Nero's confidence. A follow-up visit to the vet confirmed that Nero was going to be fine. The vet recommended that the dog not be worked for several days. Back home again, Nero gradually regained his normal activity. Randy decided to follow the vet's advice and kept Nero at home for a week. He had a few days of duty without Nero. He was astonished at how much he had grown to depend on and appreciate Nero. Randy realized that officers not working with a police dog could never appreciate the bond that exists between dog and handler.

Nero returned to duty eight days after the jail explosion. The Westfield Police Department had not developed even a sniff of a lead on who blew up the jail. The two deceased Bloods were identified as petty thieves who had had a number of run-ins with the law. The rank and file police officers applauded Nero on his return to duty. Randy felt a surge of pride as he and Nero entered to Westfield Police headquarters. The guys also lightened the mood by barking playfully at Randy.

Ernie Olsen was becoming restless. He would not relax until he confirmed that the two were gone. His anxiety lessened when he read the lead story in the Westfield Times, which said: WESTFIELD JAIL EXPLOSION KILLS TWO. The story reported that the Westfield Police Department had no suspects at the present time. Ernie exhaled loudly after reading the article. Ernie indicated that he wanted to lay low for a while. They would not stay in hiding for long.

Randy and Nero settled back into a normal routine. Nero received constant encouragement from Randy. The dog handler looked fondly at his partner riding next to him in the front seat. He was amazed at how well his partner had overcome the explosion at the Westfield Police headquarters. Randy compared in his own mind how similar dogs can be to humans. He knew that Nero was fine physically; what remained to be seen was how the dog would react when faced with a hostile situation. An event at 10:30 that evening would put those concerns to rest.

Ernie and Butch had lain low for a week. They decided that sufficient time had elapsed since the jail incident. They decided to head into town and look for some action. They were about to find some.

Lacy's Saloon was a Westfield landmark. It was owned by Horace Lacy. Horace was a third-generation owner of Lacy's. His grandfather had emigrated from Ireland to escape the religious strife so prevalent and longstanding in Belfast. Lacy's was a major watering hole for Westfield's middle class. It had seen its share of rumbles over the years. Most had ended with no more injury than a black eye or two.

Randy was patrolling on a cool Saturday evening. He had been dispatched to several routine calls, which included reports of a prowler/peeping at a West Side home of a prominent female. Randy and Nero checked the perimeter of the woman's spacious home. Randy returned to the front of woman's elegant home and informed the 35-year-old, well-built woman that who ever it was was long gone.

"Thank you, Officer," said the voluptuous woman. "Is there any way I can thank you?"

Randy, somewhat embarrassed, replied, "No, ma'am. Please call again if the individual returns."

Randy was further embarrassed when the woman said, "You sure have a beautiful dog working with you. What's his name?"

Randy replied, "His name is Nero. Have a good night, ma'am." Randy smiled and walked with Nero to his black and white.

Back on patrol, Randy smiled at the episode with the "peeping tom." Harvey Rhodes had advised his students that women really like dog handlers. "Be careful out there, guys. Most women look at police dog handlers as patient, calm individuals." The class had collectively laughed at Harvey. But they seemed to understand that he was indeed serious.

Randy had settled back into patrol, again taking advantage of having the entire city to patrol. He had heard that a few of the rank and file officers had griped about having to remain in an assigned sector. He didn't let that bother him. He felt as satisfied in his present assignment as any he had previously.

Ernie Olsen and Butch Carter sidled up to the bar at Lacy's. A number of the Bloods were already in the bar. They knew that things had the potential to detonate any time Ben was on scene. They knew the drill. Nothing went down until Ben ok-ed it. Rumor had it that some Bloods in California paid the ultimate price for bucking heads with Ben Olsen. Such was the scene on this cool Saturday evening. Randy drove past Lacy's, as he had done on countless patrols. His interest was piqued at an unusually large number of motorcycles and vehicles that he spotted in front and behind Lacey's. The Bloods had concentrated towards the rear of the bar. The front and middle part of Lacy's were occupied by a combination of blue collar workers and athletic people - sort of like mixing oil and water. Regular patrons would differ somewhat in describing how Lacy's erupted into a full-fledged riot, a riot which would require Nero to quell it.

The Bloods were becoming more and more boisterous as the time approached midnight. The trouble had been building for over an hour. The restrooms were located in the rear of Lacy's, which caused the diverse patrons to literally bump into one another throughout the evening. Comments were tossed back and forth as the blue-collar folks were beginning demonstrate disdain for the large number of shaggy-looking Bloods.

A very large blue collar man leaving the restroom bumped into one of the Bloods. Before the blue-collar man could apologize, the intoxicated Hood shouted, "Hey, man, watch where the fuck you're going, you stupid hayseed!" The blue-collared individual locked eyes with the

Hood, neither one willing to back down. Several men from each group overheard the commotion at the men's room. The two men finally went about their business.

Ernie Olsen had heard the commotion. He waved the Hood involved over to his table. The Hood explained to Ernie what had transpired outside of the restroom. Ernie seethed, barely able to control his monumental temper. Peace would last for just another moment or two.

The riot started after a waiter tripped and spilled some drinks onto several of the Bloods. Lacy's, like most bars, was not very well lit. It was very difficult to see what happened unless you were staring at the waiter. The drinks on the waiter's tray included a small pitcher of beer. That pitcher landed on the table where seated was one Ernie Olsen. The splashing beer detonated the mercurial Ernie Olsen's temper. His immediate reaction was to throw the 135-pound man in the direction of the bar. The incident resulted in an immediate response from the blue-collar guys.

The blue-collar workers did not know Ernie Olsen. They saw an innocent young man trying to make a living tossed around over an accident. Their reaction was immediate. They rushed towards the table, where Ernie Olsen had reseated himself. Olsen reacted instinctively, pushing away from the table and lunging toward the gathering of blue collar drinkers. A quiet, comfortable evening erupted in to a riot. Horace reached for his cell phone and dialed 911. Olsen and the Bloods quickly gained the upper hand. They never went anywhere without guns, knives, brass knuckles, or some kind of weapon. A total of 20 individuals were engaged in the fracas.

Ernie Olsen quickly escaped through a rear door. It was his habit to hightail it when the going got serious. Olsen, like most serious gang leaders, liked to leave the dirty work to his troops. His minion, Butch Carter, followed close behind. Olsen liked to believe that all of the Bloods would keep their mouths shut, if they knew what was good for them. Carter joked to Olsen, "How are we going to handle it if more of the gang are arrested?"

Ernie replied, "I think they know how to keep their mouths shut."

Randy Thompson heard the dispatcher alerting Westfield Police about the riot at Lacy's Bar. They dispatched a number of units to the bar. Police operating directives call for officers to stay in their respective sectors until dispatched to the scene. Randy and Nero were not constrained by that policy.

Randy turned on his emergency lights and headed for Lacy's, which was quickly devolving into a rumble of epic proportion.

A police dog handler is taught to exercise extreme caution when responding to incidents like the one going down at Lacy's. He parked his cruiser a block away from Lacy's. He observed that at least six black and whites were already on scene. He checked to ensure that he had all of his required equipment prior to running towards Lacy's.

Inside, the combat continued. The Westfield Police were outnumbered about three to one. They were not able to make a dent in the combat. The riot was only 15 minutes old; it looked at though officers from surrounding agencies would be asked to help. Police officers were always willing to help. The problem was that they would require 15 minutes to make it to Lacy's.

Randy positioned himself and Nero directly across the street from Lacy's. Another concern for dog handlers during fights or riots is the safety of the dog. Dogs can't don gas masks during a melee. A thrown bottle or rock could very easily put out a dog's eyes. Nonetheless, the dog, a legal weapon, was trained to join the fray. Randy was confident of Nero's ability, as well as his own discretion.

The outnumbered Westfield officers who had responded to Lacy's were unable to get the upper hand in a timely manner. The shift sergeant called for reinforcements. The dispatcher ordered all Westfield Police units to descend on Lacy's "AS SOON AS POSSIBLE! The combatants totaled more than 40 men, as well as several females. The blue-collar folks held their own during the early moments of the ruckus. Still, the fight escalated. Several participants from each side were injured. Two had suffered serious stab wounds. The situation was intensifying. A number of combatants spilled out onto the sidewalk in front of Lacy's.

Nero was champing at the bit to wade into the action. The shift sergeant was doing his best organize the police response. He had received a small cut on his forehead. Out of the corner of his eyes he spotted Randy and Nero. The shift sergeant trotted over to the dog and handler team. The big dog recognized the shift sergeant, but given the activity, he showed his distrust by growling. The shift sergeant asked Randy if he could end the mayhem with Nero's help.

"Of course we can, Sarge." Randy's enthusiasm and confidence reassured the shift sergeant.

"OK, Randy, how should we handle this?"

Randy calmly told the shift sergeant to signal all of the police officers out of the bar. "We'll take it from there. Have the officers standby. They need to be ready to arrest these idiots. Believe me, they'll be coming out."

A police dog clearing a riot is a sight to behold. Gang riots and disturbances are difficult to disperse. Police officers have used many of the traditional methods: water cannons, mace, pepper spray, and in recent years, Tasers. Randy had total confidence in his and Nero's ability to clear up this mess. Randy reiterated to the site sergeant that the officers would have to clear out immediately when he signaled.

Randy and Nero sidled up to the business next to Lacy's. The shift sergeant communicated with his assistant behind Lacy's. Randy nodded to the shift sergeant that he was ready.

The exodus of police stunned the Bloods and blue collar combatants. Both sides had never witnessed such behavior. The pause, however, was temporary. The gang members and blue collars were back at it. Randy was ready. Nero was ready. Randy took a few seconds to reflect on some words of advice from Harvey Rhodes. "Remember guys," he told the class," you are responsible for your dogs' welfare. You must do all that you can to protect them." Harvey paused before continuing. "The most dangerous, hands down, is a riot. Unfortunately, we can't put a gas mask on the dog. Be fully aware of the situation." Lacy's bar was essentially wrecked. The owner and staff fled out the rear door shortly after the riot started. They had certainly seen some serious fights, but none at this level.

Randy, with a wired-up Nero, entered Lacy's with the big dog at half leash. Most of the combatants froze in place after observing the snarling German Shepherd. Many of the combatants made beelines for the front and rear end of Lacy's. Those individuals were arrested without resistance. Several members of each gang, however, continued the battle. Randy ordered the remaining combatants to cease fighting. Most of the eight or nine individuals still involved were so engrossed in the commotion that they basically ignored Nero.

Finally, despite Randy's best efforts, Nero got involved. A tall, heavy set member of the Bloods snapped! He looked at Randy and Nero and said, "I will kill you and your fucking mutt if you don't get out of here."

Another member of the Bloods took up a position athwart the menacing Hood. The Hood initially involved in the stare down attempted to intimidate Nero, which absolutely failed. Finally, the other Hood lunged at Randy and Nero. Randy's initial reaction was to endeavor to pull Nero away from the two Bloods. It did not work. One of the Bloods brandished a knife and lunged for Randy. The Blood endeavored to stick Randy. Simultaneously, the other lunged at Randy. They would regret their aggression.

Nero first lit into the knife-wielding Blood. The Blood dropped the knife, throwing his hands up in shock as Nero grabbed the right arm of the now-defensive thug. The second Blood also lunged for Randy. The Westfield officer was able to subdue the other Blood. Randy signaled for reinforcements, who quickly took control of the two Bloods. The Blood who had attempted to stab Randy shouted out, "I'll sue you bastards for sic-ing that damned dog on me. That is police brutality. I need to be taken to the hospital." Nero did not inflict serious injury to the Hood. In fact, he barely broke the skin of the individual's forearm.

Randy and Nero were not hurt in the melee. They received sincere congrats from the police officers gathered in front of Lacy's. The shift sergeant in particular praised Randy. "Way to go, Randy. I wouldn't believe it if I hadn't seen it. One man and dog cleared out 30 to 40 idiots in just a few minutes. It was amazing, just amazing."

Randy thanked the shift sergeant. "You know what is so satisfying about this, Sarge? Nero performed exactly what he was trained to do. He did not inflict any unnecessary harm on the perp. This is a tremendous validation of Nero's training."

Randy and Nero were once again front-page news in Westfield. The Westfield Times again ran a bold print about the incident: WESTFIELD K-9 TEAM BREAKS UP RIOT. Randy read the paper when he awoke at 3 PM the following afternoon. Sue Thompson again fielded a torrent of congratulatory calls. She was so proud of her husband! Randy and Sue reread the article. Sue told Randy "I'm going to start a scrap book if you continue to clean up all of the bad guys in Westfield." Randy thanked his wife and replied, "I'm sure that we have a lot of work in front of us."

Ernie Olsen indeed knew that more hard times were in store for Westfield police. He railed against Randy and Nero in particular. "The damned cop and dog have to go. We have too much opportunity in this hick town." He told Butch Carter to observe Randy Thompson. "Find out where that dog cop lives. We need to take him out. Maybe some action against that pretty wife of his will cool him down."

Randy and Sue Thompson made an overnight trip to a lake approximately 50 miles south of Westfield. Randy was extremely pleased with the way things were going with Nero. The Thompsons, of course, took Nero with them on their overnight trip. Nero was like a part of Randy's life. Sue Thompson understood the bond between her husband and the dog. Moreover, the dog was far too valuable to leave alone or with a neighbor. Several neighbors had volunteered to care for Nero. In addition, Nero was a legal weapon. Nero seemed to enjoy the night off. His only purpose in life was to please and protect Randy.

Randy's first day back involved a demonstration. Harvey Rhodes stressed the value of police dogs as far as public relations. Harvey told the class "civil, state, and military outfits utilize dogs for public relations. Police dog handlers can make considerable PR points with their dogs." Randy and Nero would be "performing" in front Westfield High School juniors and seniors. Civilian and military units use the demos as a recruiting device. Sommersville dog handler Bob Walsh was again happy to serve as agitator for the demo. Randy ran Nero through the basic obedience and controlled aggression exercises. The Westfield juniors and seniors applauded graciously. Several students commented on how much more impressive it was seeing it in person. With the demo over, Randy asked if anyone had any questions.

One particularly erudite student asked Randy if he could give the audience a brief history of the use of dogs. Randy, like all police dog handlers, love it when he/she can talk up the history of dogs in security or police work. Randy then proceeded to give a 15-minute talk on canine use in security and law enforcement. The class' genuine interest in the program was very refreshing.

"Thank you for your interest. I'll try to condense it, since, as you see, dogs have been aiding humans for centuries." The students moved to the edge of their seats, not wanting to miss anything. Randy proceeded to speak, uninterrupted, for 20 minutes. He weaved a chronological masterpiece. Randy explained how cavemen fed dogs, who learned that cavemen would feed them if they hung around the cave entrance and barked at other cave dwellers or animals. Images found in caves prove that the cave dogs were the earlier forerunner to "sentry dogs". Randy pointed out how Napoleon Bonaparte utilized dogs to protect his forts by training vicious dogs to attack. Those dogs were then chained around the forts. His adversaries would have to deal with the dogs before even thinking of surmounting the walls. Randy went on to highlight how Romans had adorned dogs with spikes and sent them into battle. The students' interest in Randy's subject was obvious.

Randy shifted his lecture to modern times. "During World War I the Germans and Russians utilized thousands of dogs, primarily for installation defense and attack. The United States and its allies used very few dogs. World War II saw the Japanese, Germany, and Italy utilize thousands of dogs. The United States of America finally entered the police/sentry dog field on May 9, 1942 when a civilian firm, Dogs For Defense, demonstrated dogs trained to attack and perform sentry duty. The United States used a token number of dogs until the end of World War II. We utilized dogs in Korea; the terrain, however, limited their use and effectiveness."

Randy continued," The initial use of dogs commenced in the 1950's when sentry dogs were utilized extensively by The United States Air Force strategic air command to protect B52 bombers. The sentry dogs were limited to guard dog duty. The current 'patrol dog' evolved in the late 1960s when the Washington Metropolitan Police demonstrated patrol dogs to the United States Air Force at Lackland Air Force Base, San Antonio, Texas. The patrol dog, unlike the sentry dog, was trained to attack only when commanded to by the dog handler. The patrol dog greatly increased the visibility of police dogs. Few people would argue that police dogs provide a huge psychological advantage. Moreover, patrol dogs provided services like escorts of money, and tracking down lost people or fugitives. And like our program today, police dogs serve as a highly valuable recruitment tool."

Once again, Randy was pleased with the students' interest. Randy's final topic dealt with explosive and narcotic detector dogs. He continued, "Once again, the Washington Metropolitan Police provided instruction. The basic principle is simple: teach dogs to search for explosives or narcotics by using a highly positive reward system. The most common reward for a detector dog is a hard rubber ball or rolled up towel. The dog is trained to respond to the odor of explosives or narcotic. Narcotic detector dogs are trained to actively scratch or bite at the 'source' of the odor. Explosive detector dogs, for obvious reasons, are trained to get as close to the 'source' as possible, then to sit…for obvious reasons."

Randy opened a question and answer session. Student asked numerous questions. Among them were: why does the Department of Defense use the German Shepherd as it's primary dog? Randy explained that the German Shepherd dog provided a combination stability, moderate aggression, and olfactory ability. The demo went so well that he had to cut the program when the students had to attend their next class. The faculty thanked Randy profusely.

Ernie Olsen becoming restless. In fact, he was beyond restless. He c not anticipate the push back he was experiencing. He railed to Butch Carter and the rest of the Bloods: "We should have this hick town wrapped up by now. That's why I left LA. Out there you can't do a fucking thing without having to pay tribute to the gang." Ernie hesitated before continuing. We need to get our act in gear. The first order of business is getting rid of that dog and his cop handler!"

Randy and Nero returned to work at 8 PM the day following his presentation. The Westfield High School principal had fired off a very effusive encomium and indicated that he hoped that the dog handler would come back again in the future. Randy also received an "attaboy" from Chief Benson. Randy's first night back was uneventful. It gave him an opportunity to reflect on the first four months working with Nero. They had been instrumental in defusing several serious crimes. Moreover, Randy was surprised by the reception he and Nero had received. If the reception was an indication, he saw nothing but good things ahead. Nero's next opportunity to shine would really turn any doubters into believers.

Respect for Nero would continue to rise. A huge explosive rocked downtown Westfield at 1PM one week following the school demonstration. Randy was sound asleep, having worked until 4 AM. Randy had always been a sound sleeper. The explosion was so strong that it woke him and caused Nero to bark several times. Sue Thompson also heard the explosion. She was grocery shopping at Martel's when the explosion brought Westfield to a stop.

structure was crumbling. Miller's department store's gas lines were failing.

Several employees and customers had expressed to management they smelled gas. The current Miller running the store usually thanked the person reporting the leak with a promise to have it checked. His procrastination would have devastating consequences.

Miller's Department Store had an unusually large number of customers for a weekday. None of the customers or employees had experienced anything even remotely similar to what happened at 1PM. The natural gas was concentrated near the rear of the department store. No one would ever know what sparked the explosive. The result would be the loss of four lives. 11 people were either dead or buried beneath a huge pile of rubber that was Miller's Department Store. Nero would once again be called upon to demonstrate his phenomenal abilities.

Westfield's Fire and Police Department's responded immediately. What they saw upon arriving would remain with them for the rest of their lives. Miller's Department was a stand-alone building. The building was two stories high. The second floor consisted of two apartments. A total of six persons occupied the two apartments. Both apartments were unoccupied at the time of the explosion.

Nero was awakened by the explosion. He was standing beside Randy's bed when his handler sat up in his bed. The big dog seemed to know that the explosion was significant. It was as though he realized that they would be involved. Randy didn't have to wait to be called in. He quickly donned a uniform, gathered his gear, and ran out the door with an excited Nero close behind. One advantage of canine work was a take home squad car. He was able to see the smoke from the explosion. He turned on his emergency lights and sped to the scene.

Randy parked his police cruiser two blocks from the scene amongst several other police vehicles. He reluctantly left Nero in his cruiser. He had no reference or experience in this type of incident. His instinct told him to run to the command center for his assignment. The command center sergeant told Randy and another handful of officers to stand by. They were unable to commence a search of Miller's Department Store until Westfield Gas and Electric cut off the gas feed. The Westfield Fire Department was finally given the green light to extinguish several fires still burning. Chief Elmer Benson had arrived on scene and took control of the operation.

Randy was assigned to search the west side of the rubble that was Miller's Department Store. He hesitated just a bit. He thought of reminding Chief Benson that Nero was available. Randy thought better of mentioning Nero to a very busy Chief Benson. He didn't have to. The chief spotted Randy as the dog handler walked towards his assignment. "Thompson," yelled the chief, "I want to ask you a question. Do you think your dog could help locate anyone trapped in there?"

Randy replied, "Chief, Nero isn't a cadaver dog. He can, however, respond to human scent of live persons. I am confident he can respond to both alive and deceased scents." Chief Benson instructed Randy to retrieve Nero and stand by.

Westfield Gas and Electric were able to confirm that the gas was turned off. They suggested that first responders wait for 15 minutes to allow the gas to dissipate. The gas and electric folks also reminded first responders to refrain from smoking, for obvious reasons. The utility company personnel were satisfied that the wreckage that had been Miller's was safe, and that the search for survivors could commence. The search commenced at 1:50 PM, roughly 55 minutes after the explosion. Randy did as directed by Chief Benson - he stood by.

Westfield firefighters and police began searching for survivors. Unlike many large cities, the Westfield fire and police worked well together. They searched feverishly for survivors and deceased. The prodigious pile of rubble presented a daunting challenge. Mayor Johnson arrived on scene shortly after hearing the explosion. City Hall was just two blocks from what used to be Miller's Department Store. The mayor conferred with Chief Benson about how he could help. Johnson was a very astute and sensible man. He knew that Chief Benson was entirely capable of handling a major incident like the Miller catastrophe. Chief Benson asked the mayor to deal with the media. Mayor Johnson immediately corralled the reporters and moved them to a safe distance.

The responders were now joined by a number of citizens. The work was tedious and taxing. Randy was champing at the bit to get involved with Nero. He would soon get his wish. Chief Benson signaled for Randy to come over to the command site. Randy told Nero, "Let's go, boy, it's time to get involved." Chief Benson asked Randy how Nero could locate persons trapped in the rubble. Randy explained to the chief the specific differences between a police dog and a cadaver dog. He related that cadaver dogs are generally limited to searching for deceased persons. The police dogs, on the other hand, are taught a variety of skills: obedience, building search, tracking, controlled aggression, and field scouting. Randy told the chief that cadaver dogs are superior to police dogs when searching disasters like this. "Let me take Nero around the wreckage. He may be able to pinpoint any surviving persons." The chief told Randy to go for it!

Chief Benson escorted Randy and Nero to the command center. The chief instructed the sergeants to pull all of the responders off the rubble. Chief Benson told the officers that Randy and Nero were going to search for survivors. Several Westfield firefighters and police officers mumbled under their breath that it would be an error to count on the dog. Chief Benson glared at them, his ire apparent.

Randy proceeded to the north side of the collapsed building. A check of the wind told Randy that the wind was south to north, which would carry any scents to the north side of the rubble. Randy took Nero to the north side of the collapsed building. The scent of any person, dead or alive, would be carried south to north. Randy sat Nero down, and proceeded to reconfirm the wind direction. Satisfied that it was still south to north, he commenced the search by telling Nero to "Find 'em, boy!"

Nero looked at Randy, somewhat perplexed. The big German Shepherd was looking at Randy, a puzzled expression in his eyes. Nero was looking at an entirely foreign sight. He then looked at Randy for reassurance. Randy reached down to pet the dog, telling him, "It's okay, big boy. Let's go to work." With that reassurance, Nero began to ingest larger than normal amounts of air.

Miller's Department Store was a cinder block structure building. A steel framed building would present more jagged edges. Moreover, a brick or cinder block structure would result in larger piles of debris. The large pile of rubble would also muffle cries from persons trapped. First responders had endeavored to hear any crying persons trapped in the large rubble. They were unable to detect the persons trapped, if indeed there were survivors. Nero would once again demonstrate his abilities.

Seven people were trapped in the rubble. A family of four had survived the blast. They were near the front of Miller's paying for merchandise. Two employees and a middle-aged woman had also survived in the middle of the department store. The seven trapped persons were emitting copious amounts of human scent. That scent was affected by gravity. When the scent hit ground level, it dispersed.

The scent slowly drifted towards the north end of the rubble. Randy worked Nero around the rubble in an endeavor to see if he could pick up a scent emanating from the rubble. Minute amounts of the scent were beginning to matriculate towards Nero. Randy, like all good dog handlers, studied his dog's behavior as it began its search. Dog handlers are trained to closely watch their dogs during any type of search. Randy had already conditioned himself, as dog handlers have for years, "to look where the dog looks." Nero hadn't alerted on human scent; he did, however, seem to be interested in the gigantic pile of rubble. Randy felt confident that these indicators would result in locating the trapped persons, presuming there were survivors.

Paul Carson, his wife, Erin, and children, Paul Jr, and Lisa, were trapped under a 4X4 inch wooden beam. Paul Carson realized that the 4X4 blocking their escape had saved their lives. Paul knew that he had to reassure his family that they would be rescued very soon. None of the Carsons was seriously injured. Erin and Paul Jr. suffered several cuts. Paul Carson did his best he could to remain calm; he also realized that help would be a long time getting to them. He was extremely proud of his family.

Nero searched in a more confident manner in just a few minutes. The unsteady footing initially caused him to proceed cautiously. The big dog was locked in to his task: find any persons trapped under this huge pile of rubble. Randy did all that he could to protect Nero against nails and splinters. The unsteady footing spooked the dog but still, he pressed on. The cornucopia of scents presented Nero with a challenging task. The rubble itself was difficult enough. Added to that was the variety of scents emanating from the huge pile of rubble. Along with the building materials, Nero was barraged by the scent of merchandise, gas, and of course, human scent.

Beneath the large pile of debris, the Paul Carson family was hanging on. The Carson children were beginning to manifest impatience. Paul Carson endeavored to reassure the children and his wife. The enormity of Miller's Department Store rubble seemed to Paul to be too large to allow a timely rescue. The Carson family had given up on shouting for help. Paul asked his family to cease yelling and to conserve energy.

The collective odor of the Carson family, the three other survivors, and the remains of the four deceased persons was beginning to move. The majority of that scent drifted towards the northern end of the rubble. Nero had elevated his intensity. He had presented several "peculiar" alerts. A peculiar alert or response happens when a dog is presented with a series of scents, including the subjects of the search. Randy had studied Nero closely and knew how the big dog reacted to various olfactory challenges. The combination of debris, gas, survivors, and the deceased presented Nero with a significant challenge.

Chief Benson, Mayor Johnson, firefighters, newspeople, and onlookers watched as Randy led Nero through the rubble. The onlookers were unanimous in the opinion that no one could survive the explosion. Among them was Gene Callaway, the Westfield Fire Chief. Callaway openly questioned the mayor and Chief Benson's decision to allow Randy and Nero the first crack at the rescue of any survivals. "We're wasting precious time," Callaway said, to no one in particular. Chief Benson replied to Callaway that they would allow Randy a few more minutes before pulling the dog/handler team.

Nero, although somewhat unsteady on the rubble, stopped suddenly and planted his nose into a crevice approximately one-third up the south end of the rubble. Randy Thompson knew instantly that Nero was indicating where survivors were buried. The onlookers could plainly see that Nero had indicated the presence of human beings. The crowd of onlookers moved closer to the rubble as Nero remained locked down on the scent emanating from the rubble.

Randy waved to Chief Benson, who trotted quickly to Randy and Nero's position on the large pile that was formerly Miller's Department Store. "Chief," said Randy, "have the searchers concentrate here through this narrow space. They're buried straight back from here." Chief Benson had learned to trust Randy and Nero. Benson hollered for Fire Chief Calloway, who was talking with his fire captains. Calloway walked slowly to where Chief Benson was talking to Randy and several cops.

"Chief," said Benson to Calloway, "We need to concentrate our efforts through this slight opening here."

Calloway grunted, "10-4."

Police, firefighters, and a phalanx of volunteers began the recovery process. Nero's pinpoint indication of the family saved valuable time. Responders were able to hear the Carson family. The three other victims, significantly closer to the north end, were rescued with little difficulty. Although closer to the responders, the three were too traumatized to yell for help. The gentleman trapped with the other two ladies suffered a broken leg. All three received cuts and bruisers, none serious. Mayor Johnson and Chiefs Benson and Calloway spoke briefly with the trio, who were very appreciative of the responders' effort. The city officials knew that a more significant challenge lie ahead.

Randy had taken Nero home where he briefed Susan prior to returning to help with the rescue. The city moved a front-end loader to assist with the recovery. Responders and city maintenance worked feverishly to free the Carson family. The Carson family was rescued at 5 PM, approximately four hours after the explosion. They had been very fortunate to have suffered no serious injuries. It would take them some time. Chiefs Benson and Calloway spoke to Paul Carson, who was most appreciative of the police, firefighters, and volunteers. Chief Benson signaled Randy to come join them.

"Sir," said Chief Benson, "this young officer's dog told us where to search. We would still be looking for you if it weren't for this officer and his dog."

Paul Carson thanked Randy, then asked where Nero was. Randy responded, "Sir, I took Nero home after he pinpointed your location so I could assist with the rescue." Mr. Carson then asked if he and his family could meet Nero.

Chief Benson replied, "I'm pretty sure that we can arrange that. But let's get you to the hospital."

Ernie Olson was cruising around the streets of Westfield with Butch Carter, looking for action, when he saw the commotion around Miller's Department Store. Curiosity got the best of Ernie and Butch. They parked a block or so away from Miller's. They asked a uniformed police officer what the commotion was all about. The uniformed officer, who did not recognize the Bloods, replied, "Gas explosion. A number of folks were killed. Some trapped people were rescued. A police dog was able to point out where the trapped folks were. Saved their lives." Ernie thanked the officer and signaled for Butch to follow him.

"What's going on, boss? Why did we leave the cop so fast?"

Ernie looked at Butch and said, "This is why I'm in charge and you're not! If the cop and that damned dog are here, who's home watching over his old lady?"

Butch looked at Ernie and replied, "Wait a minute, you're not thinking what I think you are?"

"You better believe I am," replied Ernie Olsen. "All of those cops are down there at the explosion. That's why I had you find out that dog cop's address. We're going to go over there and snatch up that cop's lady."

With the survivors transported to Westfield General, the emphasis turned to the recovery of the deceased. Two women and two men were crushed when a large support beam fell on them. They had the misfortune to be standing directly above the leaking gas line. Family members of the deceased were comforted by relatives and friends. They ranged from 26-45 years of age. Family members had responded to Miller's, demanding answers for the explosion. Mayor Johnson and Chief Benson assured the family members that a full, comprehensive investigation would be completed. The mayor and chief headed back to headquarters, where TV and newspaper reporters were waiting. Chief Benson instructed Randy to remain close by, as the reporters would no doubt want to interview him.

Sue Thompson had been glued to the TV. Once again, Randy and Nero had performed in an outstanding manner. Nero sat on the Thompson sofa with Sue. Sue told Nero, "See all of that commotion, boy! All of those people are talking about you!" Sue could barely control her pride. She knew how fulfilling Randy's job had become for him. The following 12 hours or so would once again demonstrate how valuable Nero was.

Ernie Olsen and Butch Carter cruised by the Thompson household. They saw no additional vehicles parked near Randy and Sues home. Ernie was under the impression that Nero was with Randy at police headquarters. Ernie explained the plan to Butch Carter. "We'll knock on the front door. When she answers, we'll just overpower her and take her out of town. Her old man is downtown."

Butch Carter gave Ernie a skeptical look. "Okay, boss. If you think so. Let's do it!"

Sue Thompson relaxed on her sofa. She had opened the kitchen door to let Nero outside. She stretched out on the sofa. She could not wait for Randy to get home. She was hoping for a little private time with her hero husband. The knock at the front door didn't alarm her. She assumed it was a friend or neighbor wanting to talk about the explosion and how Nero had saved those lives. She saw through the security peephole that two unknown men were standing on the front door porch.

Randy had drilled into Sue that she should never open their door for a stranger. Nevertheless, she opened the front door without hesitation. Olsen and Carter were on her in an instant. They wore masks to hide their identity. They tied and gagged her with rope they had brought with them. They also wore masks until they had her blindfolded. Their plan was to move Olsen's vehicle inside the Thompson's garage where they would load her into the rear seat and abscond out of town. Olsen sent Carter out to move their vehicle into the Thompson's garage. Olsen moved Sue into the garage where he had her open the garage doors. Butch Carter eased Olsen's car into the garage. The two thugs forced Sue into the back seat of the vehicle, warning her to keep her trap shut. Nero, playing with neighbor's dog by running along the fence line, did not hear the commotion inside.

Butch Carter eased into the front passenger seat while Ernie Olsen walked behind the vehicle prior to taking the driver's seat. He almost made it. The Thompson home did not have a doggie door. Nero was simply too large. Randy Thompson had developed a system for Nero wherein the dog could gain entrance to the house on his own. He tied a piece of rope to the garage back door. It was easy to teach Nero to pull open the door without disturbing Randy and Sue.

Estimates of a dog's hearing vary. Conventional wisdom says that dogs can hear up to 200 times better than humans. One stark reality is this: dogs have an astonishing advantage over humans regarding hearing. Sue Thompson fought valiantly to avoid being forced into the vehicle. Her determination did not prevent her abduction; however, the commotion did reach Nero in the back yard. The big dog heard Sue Thompson's cries of resistance. It took the big dog a few seconds to assimilate the information. He then snapped into gear. Ernie Olsen had reached the rear of his vehicle when Nero pulled open the rear garage door. Olsen froze in place. Nero could hear Sue struggling inside Olsen's vehicle. The big dog lunged at Ernie Olsen, grabbing the Hood by the left leg. Olsen screamed at Carter, "Get me something I can use to get this fucking shit eater off me!!!"

Carter reached into the glove box for a set of brass knuckles he kept for emergencies. He handled it to Olsen, who proceeded to whack Nero on his nose, which caused the dog to back off.

Olsen was able to slam the driver's side door shut. He gunned the engine, leaving a bewildered, bleeding Nero standing beneath the garage door. The big dog was perplexed, unsure of what just occurred, and why Sue had left with persons unknown to him. Nero sat down in the garage, as if waiting for his owners to come home. He wouldn't have to wait long. A routine Westfield patrol officer drove past the Thompson's home. The officer immediately realized that something was amiss at the Thompson's. The garage door was open, and Nero was sitting in front of the garage. The patrol officer stopped in front of the house. He was unsure if he should approach Nero. He was tempted to check on the house, but thought better after he observed Nero staring at him. The officer did the prudent thing, calling dispatch to inform Randy what he had observed.

Randy Thompson had finally finished the paperwork necessary regarding Miller's Department Store. He was shooting the breeze with several officers when the desk sergeant interrupted him with a startling message: the garage door was open, and Nero was sitting in front of it. Randy shot out of headquarters and ran to his black and white. He fired up the engine, turned on his lights, and sped towards his home. He tried to imagine what could have transpired at his home. He knew that Nero would protect Sue. A million possibilities ran through Randy's mind as he approached his home.

Randy's heart sank when he saw Nero sitting in the garage. He jumped out of his cruiser and ran to Nero. Randy could see that Nero had sustained a significant injury to his nose. After reassuring Nero, he ran into his home yelling for Sue. Randy searched frantically for Sue, Nero at his side. He sank to his knees momentarily torn between fear for Sues' safety and rage. He hurried back to the front of his home, where the patrol officer reported that he had not seen anyone leaving Randy's home. Several additional units had arrived, led by Chief Benson.

The chief ordered several officers to immediately canvass the area in the hope that someone had seen anything. They hit pay dirt immediately. A senior gentleman across the street reported that he had seen a vehicle back into the Thompson's garage. He stated that it must have been okay. When the patrolman asked why, the senior said, "Simple: I knew that Nero was at home. I didn't have any reason to think that Ms. Thompson was in any jeopardy." The gentleman had gone to the restroom, and when he returned, the vehicle was gone. He could not identify the make or model of the vehicle. He was able to tell the officers that it was a four-door and dark blue or black in color.

Chief Benson comforted Randy and directed the shift sergeant to mobilize all Westfield Police Department resources to search for Sue Thompson. He also directed the desk sergeant to advise the county to be on the lookout for a vehicle described by the senior gentleman. Randy sat absolutely transfixed with rage. Nero's presence comforted Randy. The Thompson's veterinarian, Doctor Howell, checked Nero, who was sore and confused. The forensic officers checked the Thompson household with great care. They were unable to uncover any evidence relating to the disappearance. No DNA or fingerprints, not even Randy's or Sue's, were found. Randy was about to explode with rage. Chief Benson comforted Randy. "Randy, do you have any reason to believe that someone would want to hurt or take Susan?"

Randy responded, “No sir, Chief. I have no reason to think – wait a minute. It could be those thugs from the Hamby or Martel’s cases. Beyond those two incidents, nothing sticks.” The chief told Randy to stay at home. Randy protested, but the chief insisted.

“Stay here with Nero, Randy. I promise you that we will find her. I promise to call you the second we find her.”

Chapter 14

Ernie Olsen and Butch Carter, with Sue Thompson in tow, headed south of town. Ernie Olsen's leg was throbbing. He railed at no one in particular, "That damned dog fucked up my leg. I swear I am going to kill that shit-eating dog." Sue Thompson listened to Olsen with an overwhelming sense of doom. She sobbed out loud, prompting Olsen to scream, "Shut the fuck up, bitch! It's your old man and that fucking dog to thank for this. Now shut the fuck up!" Sue Thompson continued to whimper, but was able to stifle it sufficiently to keep Olsen off her – for now. She yearned to be in Randy's arms, where she always felt safe.

Randy was beside himself. He sat on his sofa with Nero sitting beside him. He could not recall a time in his life when he felt so helpless. He wondered if he was guilty of putting his career ahead of her. He glanced down at Nero, patted him gently on his head. To Randy, Nero could sense that something was amiss. Psychologists, professional trainers, and ordinary citizens were of the opinion that a dog could sense when it's owner or trainer was in distress. Finally, numerous persons have related situations where a two-dog family loses one; the second dog is really never the same. Randy hugged his big dog, thankful for having him at such a stressful time. Randy wanted to search for Sue. Two factors prevented his joining the search: Nero's injury and instructions from Chief Benson to stay home.

Ernie Olsen laughed out loud at nothing in particular. Butch Carter stared at the boss, asking what was so fucking funny.

"Butch," he said to Carter, "the reason I call the shots, son, is because of ideas like this. We're going to hold this bitch for ransom money."

Butch Carter was incredulous. "Are you serious? How the fuck are we going to pull it off?"

Ernie Olsen smiled at his companion, telling him, "I'll let you in on it in due time. Now we have to get to a remote area where I know a dude who will let us lay low with this fucking woman. Yeah, Westfield's police department is going to pay for this."

Pat Harkins had known Ernie Olsen in California. Ernie had called Harkins previously, asking him if he could hide at his house if necessary. Harkins had "made his bones" with the Bloods out West. Pat had retired several years ago with honor. He had been an "enforcer" for the Bloods. Now, at 48 years old, he wanted to relax with his woman, Cindy. Ernie found the place without difficulty. Pat ran out to Ernie's car and bear hugged Ernie, picking up the Hood leader. Pat Harkins stood 6' 5" tall and weighed 260 pounds. Pat heard a commotion emanating from Ernie's car. Ernie told Butch to fetch Sue Thompson from the car.

Pat and Cindy stared at the tied up young woman, their shock evident. Pat said, "What the fuck is going on, Ernie? Who's this woman?"

Ernie smiled and said, "She's that dog cop's old lady."

Pat related that he and Cindy had read about Nero and the dog cop. Ernie continued, "Yeah, and that fucking dog bit the shit out of my leg." Ernie showed his bitten leg to Pat and Cindy. Cindy ran to the Harkins' cabin to retrieve a First Aid kit. She cleaned up Ernie's leg wound as best she could. Cindy told Ernie that he should have it treated at a hospital. Ernie grunted a thank you to Cindy. "Thanks, lady," Ernie told her, "but that's the last thing I need. Cops will be looking for me."

The Westfield Police Department brass and rank and file were convinced that Sue Thompson was taken south by the kidnappers. Heretofore, all of the Bloods activity had been to south of town. Chief Benson instructed his sergeants to emphasize the majority of their units towards south of town. The chief also urged his officers to be very cautious when approaching any situation even remotely related to the kidnapping. "Remember, guys, they have the wife of one of our brothers. Work hard, but work smart."

Olsen had a hard time convincing Butch and Pat Harkins the he was dead serious about demanding a ransom payment for Sue Thompson.

"Bet your asses I'm serious," Olsen told them. "You're right we're going to get a large chunk of cash and then we'll blow this hick town." Butch and Pat Harkins saw that he was dead serious. Randy asked Pat to take him to a Walmart or similar market to purchase several throw away phones. Butch Carter asked Ernie how they were going to pull it off. Ernie responded, "In due time."

Randy Thompson could not sit by waiting for something to happen. He had to do something. He was always one to follow instructions, particularly when they came directly from the Westfield Chief of Police. Still, it was impossible to sit by while his wife was out there with those thugs. He gathered up Nero and his weapon and gear and headed out to look for his wife. He told himself that he could punch the life out of those sons of bitches. Randy loaded Nero into his cruiser and headed out to look for his wife. He petted Nero and told the big dog, "We're going to go find Sue." It was as though the big dog understood the gravity of the situation.

Ernie Olsen laid out the ransom plan. "We're going to set the amount for this bitch at $200,000." Butch Carter just stared at Ernie. Ernie continued, "We're going to call the police using one of those disposable phones. We're going to give them one chance and one chance only." Ernie then shared the rest of the plan. He would drive across town to place the call. That tactic, coupled with the throw away phone, would preclude the police from nailing down their position. Carter followed up with the most logical question: "What will we do if they don't come up with the bread?"

Ernie replied confidently. "We'll cross that bridge when the time comes. Rest assured that we won't go down because of the bitch in the back room!"

Sue Thompson had been held in a laundry room at the back of the Harkin's place. She had been captive for approximately three hours. They left her tied and blind folded. She had begged and pleaded to be set free. Ernie screamed, "Shut the fuck up, bitch!!"

Sue's feeling of total helplessness increased as time passed. She assumed that Randy had returned to find her missing. She also knew that the Westfield Police Department had mobilized to find her. More than anything, she knew that Randy was looking for her. She prayed that they would find her in time. They had not harmed her thus far. Still, she was terrorized.

Olsen had driven across town with the throw away cell phone. He knew that he was taking a chance. He hoped that his plan would work. He stopped at a point ten miles west of downtown Westfield. As planned, he would make it perfectly clear to the cops that the cop's wife would be killed if the city didn't comply with their demands. The Hood leader also knew that the Bloods' hierarchy in LA would hear about it and expect their share. Ernie dialed the Westfield Police Department four hours after the incident started.

Desk Sergeant Ed Norris took the call. He picked up the desk phone on the first ring. Norris had been with the Westfield Police Department for 16 years. He had, as desk sergeant, answered so many calls that he had reached a point where, in his own words, "I've taken enough calls that nothing surprises me." Norris was, however, unprepared for the call from the Hood leader.

"Westfield Police, may I help you?" Olsen hesitated, then told the desk sergeant, "Listen up. We have the dog cop's old lady. Write this down. We want $200,000 cash, all small, untraceable bills. Get it together fast. We'll call two hours from now. Tell your people that the cop's bitch is dead if you don't comply!" Norris tried to keep the caller on the phone long enough to be traced. The effort had not succeeded.

Desk Sergeant Norris immediately notified the shift supervisor who, in turn, briefed Chief Benson. The chief directed that all of the key players were to report to headquarters immediately Chief Benson asked the desk sergeant if the phone could be traced. Norris replied that the call lasted less than 30 seconds. "Probably used one of those disposable phones." The chief had the call replayed. All calls to police headquarters are taped. Chief Benson knew that the Westfield Police Department was up against a terrible criminal.

Police departments across the across the country routinely seek assistance from federal agencies, namely the Federal Bureau of Investigation. The Feds were always willing to help. Problem was that it took time to organize an operation involving different agencies. With a two-hour timeframe, Chief Benson realized that the Westfield Police Department was on its own. They had little time to save Sue Thompson.

Randy Thompson had no idea where the Bloods were holding his wife. Although not nearly as big as New York or Houston, the vast open areas adjoining the city made speculating useless. Still, he had to look for Sue. The feeling of helplessness was overwhelming. Randy castigated himself for not providing Sue with sufficient awareness of what is possible in today's world. He felt that his desire to have Sue be a housewife instead of working at a routine job contributed to her kidnapping. He reminisced how they felt that is was time for them to start a family. In fact, they were hoping that Sue had already conceived. Randy headed home after scouring the outskirts of Westfield. He knew that he had to be available should anything break regarding the search for his wife.

Chapter 15

Ernie Olsen once again took to the road to deliver the ransom details to the Westfield police. He had actually written down the message he would deliver. He didn't want any detail to be overlooked. He had seen too many stories wherein the kidnappers dragged out the operations far too long. Those incidents usually ended up with the kidnappers arrested. Ernie reasoned that a short-lived operation would favor his crew. What Olsen did not factor in was what he would do if the cops refused the ransom demand.

The call came in precisely two hours after the initial one. Chief Benson and his senior assistants were standing by, waiting for the call. The desk sergeant waved at Chief Benson, who picked up another phone to listen in. Ernie Olsen cut to the chase. "Listen up, cop. I'm only going to tell you the plan one time. Screw it up and the bitch is dead."

Desk Sergeant Ed Norris replied, "Yes, sir." Chief Benson and the desk sergeant looked at each other.

Once again, Olsen spoke, "Here's what you pigs are going to do. You have one hour to leave $200,000 in cash, all $20s and $50s. Deposit the money in the dumpster behind the Westfield Diner. No tricks. If we even smell a cop, she's dead." The phone went dead.

Chief Benson sprang into action. He called the President of the Westfield National Bank. He laid out the situation to Wesley Donaldson, president of the city's largest bank.

"Wow, Chief, that's a lot of cash."

The chief responded, "Look here, Wesley, these guys have Officer Thompson's wife. They said they will kill her if we don't pony up the cash."

Wesley Donaldson knew that he had no choice. "Give me a few minutes to call some of the board members to see how they feel about this. That's a lot of money."

Chief Benson pounded on the desk. "We don't have time, Wesley! I'll take responsibility for the money."

Chief Benson, with money in hand, sped back to headquarters. He briefed his officers of the plan he had devised while driving back from the bank. "We'll drop off the money behind the diner. I want plainclothes people stationed strategically near the diner. Sergeant Norris will handle the assignments. Make damned sure that we have no black and whites in view. Let's get on this. Remember, they have Randy's wife."

The galvanized police officers, led by Chief Benson, set about their grim task. The chief wrestled with whether or not to inform Randy of the impending operation. He thought better of it. The chief could not prevent Westfield Police Officer Brent Sullivan from calling Randy Thompson, filling in the grieving officer of the ransom demand.

Randy thanked Sullivan, promising to keep his mouth shut regarding the heads up on the ransom. He once again loaded up a high-strung Nero. Randy knew that getting involved was counter to the instructions laid down by Chief Benson. He could not just sit still, particularly knowing where the money drop would be. He was having trouble assimilating all of the information he had received. The dog handler was very aware of the peril that can surface when a police officer is involved in difficult situations involving family members. Nevertheless, he could not stand by at home while his wife's life was on the line.

The Westfield Diner had been doing very well. The dinner hour crowd was beginning to thin out. Approximately ten patrons were still eating dinner when the unmarked car pulled up to the rear of the Westfield Dinner. The driver slowed down to scope out the area before stopping next to the trash dumpster. He hesitated for a few seconds. He then calmly exited the vehicle, walked directly to the dumpster, and lowered the satchel containing the ransom money into the dumpster. The officer then returned to the unmarked vehicle and drove slowly away.

Ernie Olsen had mapped out his plan to retrieve the money. Typically, he would isolate himself from the action. He dispatched Butch Carter and another Hood to Westfield to retrieve the cash. Ernie Olsen had lectured them to be alert for cops. He emphasized that they must avoid getting snagged. The plan called for Carter to drop off the other Hood about two blocks from the Westfield Diner. When the subordinate Hood was satisfied that the coast was clear, he was to snatch up the satchel and walk south of the bank calmly until Carter would pick him up.

Randy, with an energized Nero, positioned his cruiser in an alley two blocks south of the Westfield Diner. He knew that the Westfield Police Department had stationed unmarked units in key positions with a clear sight line to the bank. All of the police units could clearly see the bank president drop the satchel into the dumpster. Ernie had cautioned them to allow a few minutes before retrieving the satchel. "We need to be as inconspicuous as possible. Make damned sure that you don't get snagged. If you do, keep your fucking mouth shut."

Ernie Olsen and Pat Harkins knocked back a few beers while they waited for Butch to return with the cash.

"Pat," said Ernie, "I'll make sure to take care of you and Cindy for helping us out. You guys have got to button up over this. Kidnapping is a federal offense. Remember, there is no parole with them."

Harkins responded sarcastically, "What woman?"

They both yukked it up over that joke. Ernie was more nervous than he showed.

Harkins then asked the biggest question of all: "What about the broad? What ya going to do with her?"

Ernie threw a wicked glance at Ernie. "You dumbass, if you hadn't noticed, we have her blindfolded."

Butch Carter, ebullient over the pile of cash in the satchel, was laughing outwardly, showing little concern for remaining inconspicuous. Carter shouted out loud, "Man, we pulled it off! Ernie is going to love it, man!"

They had made it to the outskirts of town when Carter committed a blunder of epic proportions. Ernie Olsen's right hand man, so excited, dialed Ernie's cell phone. Ernie Olsen almost jumped out of his clothes when he recognized Butch Carter's number on his cell phone. "That fucking idiot just told the cops where we are! I can't believe how stupid that son of a bitch is!"

Chief Benson signaled to the shift sergeant to take down the vehicle heading out of town. Three units quickly took down Carter and the other Hood, along with the money. Chief Benson himself pulled up on the scene of the takedown. The shift sergeant was already reading the two Bloods their Miranda Rights when Chief Benson walked up to the scene. He observed as the shift sergeant completed the formalities. A good chief would never interrupt one of his men while conducting police business. With the formalities over, Chief Benson asked the shift sergeant if he could speak to the two men.

Carter laughed at the chief. "If you think I'm going to give you anything, you're nuts."

Chief Benson then delivered a crushing blow to Carter. "Let me tell you something. We have already triangulated the position of your gang. Who's laughing now? Take them away." The chief directed his officers to secure the ransom money.

Ernie paced the floor like an expectant father. Pat and Cindy asked Ernie what they were going to do.

Ernie Olsen hesitated before responding. "We'll give it 10 or 15 minutes. If they're not back, I'll snatch the woman up and hit the road with her. It will be as though we were never here. Thanks for helping out, Pat. I'll make it up to you some day."

Sue Thompson was not going to give up without a fight. She had managed to remove the blindfold and was working on the ropes tying her hands behind her. She had nearly succeeded when Ernie Olsen walked into the room. She froze in place, unable to move. Olsen looked at her in disbelief. "What the fuck are you doing?"

Already angry over Carter's blunder, Ernie lost it. He slapped Sue twice, his anger continuing to grow.

The game had flipped over for Ernie Olsen. Ernie realized that he had few options. The cop's woman had seen his face. She would have to go. He was not going to prison because this woman had seen his face. He stood over Sue Thompson. The fear in her eyes was evident. She pleaded with Olsen. "Please! Let me go! I swear to you that I will not tell anyone who you are, please!"

Randy was sitting in his cruiser with Nero when the desk sergeant notified all units of the cell phone pings generated by Carter's phone call to Olsen. He quickly pulled up the coordinates on his computer. Randy was familiar with the area. He had been involved in a number of incidents close to where his wife was being held. He didn't care about the chief's direction to remain at home. He headed south, lights and sirens engaged. Randy had a head start on the rest of the Westfield Police Department units. He hoped that he could make it to the grid indicated by the cell tower.

Ernie Olsen determined that the woman had to go. He had retied the ropes behind Sue Thompson to a point that she felt her circulation would be impeded. She was too terrified to complain. Olsen had cut her lip and bruised her cheek when he hit her. She had little doubt that this man would kill her. She thought of Randy and her family. She was so proud of her husband. Sue had no reservations about her husband's career. She loved him deeply. The despair she felt was total. Sue realized that she may not ever see her husband again.

Randy approached the county road several miles south of Westfield. Several county units, unaware of the situation, waved at Randy, who ignored them completely. They quickly took off after Randy and Nero. They called in to their dispatcher who filled them in on why Westfield PD was barreling north into the county. They informed their dispatcher that they were available for any assistance needed.

Olsen dragged Sue Thompson out of Harkins' place, and forced her into the back of his car. Olsen stared at her and told in a very menacing tone, "Listen up, bitch. You had better lay on the floor. If you even whimper, I will blow your fucking brains out."

Sue lay on the floor, too gripped with fear to even cry. Olsen said a hasty goodbye to Pat and Cynthia Harkins prior to jumping into his vehicle and heading north. For Sue Thompson, each mile only served to increase her sense of foreboding.

Randy Thompson had missed Olsen and Sue by 20 minutes. The GPS indicated to Randy that he was maddeningly close to his wife. Each passing moment multiplied his desperation. Randy drove for about one mile in this sparsely-populated area. He happened upon a dusty road where he observed what appeared to be fresh tire tracks. He turned left onto the dusty road. It led directly to a single home where Randy was met by a couple, the Harkins. Pat Harkins approached Randy's black and white, jumping back when he saw Nero in the back seat.

"Evening, Officer, can I help you?"

Randy told Nero to "Stay" prior to exiting his cruiser.

Randy shook Pat Harkins' hand before speaking to him. "Possibly. We're looking for an individual who has kidnapped a lady. We believe he may headed this way." Randy noticed that the individual appeared to be extremely nervous.

Pat Harkins responded, "No, sir. Do you know what kind of vehicle he was driving?"

Randy replied, noticing that this individual was becoming even more rattled, "All we know is that it's a dark colored sedan, 4-door."

Harkins replied that they had not seen any vehicle matching that description. Randy was certain that this individual knew something. He decided to try a trick taught to him by Harvey Rhoads.

"Sir," said Randy, "I hate to bother you, but would you mind if I use your restroom? Been on the road for a while."

Harkins responded "By all means, Officer. Cynthia, will show you where the restroom is?"

Harvey Rhodes had taught the class that dog handlers could get around obstacles by using their heads. Randy then told the Harkins that he would have to take Nero with him, a standard regulation. Pat Harkins once again almost fell all over himself, telling Randy that it would not be a problem.

"Thanks again," said Randy. He followed Cynthia Harkins into the Harkins' residence. She went back outside to join her husband. Randy was hoping she would do just that.

Nero was very familiar with Sue Thompson's scent. That is one advantage canine officers have with take home dogs. The scents of the handler and his/her family become ingrained in the dog's memory bank. Randy again thought of his dog's incomparable olfactory ability. He went into the restroom with Nero. Randy hesitated for about one minute before exiting the restroom with Nero. He was pleased to see that Pat and Cynthia Harkins were still outside, waiting for him. He took a shot at it, unleashing

Nero and telling him, "Find him, boy." Nero immediately began a systematic search of the one-story home. It took him all of 30 seconds to begin to scratch and bark at a small laundry room just off the kitchen.

Dog handlers have the ability to read their dogs responses. In the lexicon of dog handlers, the dog doesn't "alert" on a person, narcotic, or explosive. Instead, they "respond" to those stimuli. Randy was positive that Sue Thompson had been in this room. He had to act swiftly. He knew that whomever took Sue had a head start. He had to confront these people. He snapped Nero onto his leash and headed outside to confront the Harkins. A most propitious circumstance occurred as another Westfield unit pulled up to the Harkins driveway.

Pat and Cynthia Harkins were standing in front of their home, smoking cigarettes. They seemed to be nonplussed as Randy and Nero exited through the front door. Randy pulled no punches with the Harkins. "Listen, you two, I know that one of the Bloods was here with a woman. Let me tell you right now that if you don't fess up to me right now, you will be looking at prison for harboring fugitives. And by the way, that woman is my wife."

Cynthia Harkins immediately caved. She shouted at Pat Harkins, "I told you that you should have run him off when he arrived! Look at the mess we're in now!"

Randy interrupted Cynthia, "Listen, you two can settle your personal crap later. When did they leave?"

Pat Harkins, aware that he was would be in major trouble for harboring a kidnapper, volunteered. "They left about 15 to 20 minutes ago."

An incredulous Randy screamed at the Harkins, asking which way they went and what Olsen was driving. Harkins relayed that they drove off into the night. Randy surmised that Olsen had driven north, as he had not witnessed any vehicles driving south. Randy loaded Nero into his cruiser after asking the county boys to detain the Harkins until he returned.

Ernie Olsen drove north, anxious to leave Westfield in his rearview mirror. Sue Thompson continued to whimper on the floor of the vehicle, directly behind Olsen. The Hood chieftain was growing more agitated as he continued fleeing Westfield. He knew that he had to decide what to do with the cop's wife. Olsen also knew that he could not get away while dragging the woman along with him.

Randy turned north, lights ablaze, as he raced to close the gap between the fleeing Hood and himself. He drove so fast that he almost lost control of his cruiser. He slowed down slightly after telling himself that he could not find Sue if he wrecked his cruiser. Traffic was light, which made his pursuit somewhat easier. The terrain thinned out as he continued north out of Westfield's suburbs. He could hear the sirens and see the lights of both Westfield police and county sheriff. Randy flew by several vehicles that had moved to the shoulder to allow him to pass. Then, in the distance, Randy saw a glow several miles ahead. From that distance, it was plain to see that an automobile had crashed and was burning. An immeasurable sense of gloom and foreboding overcame Randy Thompson.

He rolled up on the vehicle, dreading what could be the most tragic incident of his life. Instinct told him that Sue was in the burning vehicle. He left a very nervous and agitated Nero in his cruiser. Randy then opened the trunk of his cruiser, retrieved a fire extinguisher, and dashed to the burning vehicle. The fire was confined primarily to the engine compartment. Randy was able to extinguish the fire in short order. Several city and county units pulled up on the scene as Randy opened the right rear passenger door of the smoldering vehicle. To his horror, he discovered Sue on the floor of the vehicle, gasping for air.

Randy and a county officer gently pulled Sue Thompson out of the vehicle. The dedicated police dog handler slumped to the ground next to his wife. Randy's emotions ran the gamut of grief and anger. The anger was trumped by the fear. The Westfield Police Department shift sergeant took over. His first order of business was to transport Sue Thompson to the Westfield General Hospital. Randy was hovering over the officers attending to Sue. The shift supervisor gently led Randy away from Sue.

"Randy," said the sergeant, "let the guys take care of her."

Randy, who was about to explode with anger and grief, told the sergeant to take care of her. "I'm taking Nero out to nail the son of a bitch who did this to Sue!"

"Listen, Randy," said the sergeant, "you are going to the hospital with your wife. We'll find the SOB who did this."

"Thanks, Sarge," said Randy, "I'll take off and drop off Nero at home."

"Listen, Randy," said the shift sergeant, "I think Nero knows me well enough for me to take him home. Just give me your house and cruiser keys."

The shift sergeant walked with Randy to the dog handler's cruiser. Nero immediately recognized the sergeant. Randy opened the door to allow Nero to bound out. The shift sergeant bent over and greeted Nero as though they were old friends. "I guess it will be all right," Randy mused as he petted Nero and handed his leash to the sergeant. The dog handler walked over to Sue, who was being carefully loaded into a county police van. Randy was experiencing emotion unlike any he had before in his life. He once again questioned his choice to become a dog handler. He felt selfish. He also struggled to control a rising anger. He once again chastised himself for not concentrating on his critically injured wife. He knelt down and took her hands. His fellow officers consoled him as best they could.

The police convoy headed towards Westfield with sirens and lights blaring. They made it to Westfield General Hospital in 15 minutes. The emergency room staff was standing by when the convoy pulled up. Sue was placed on a stretcher and wheeled into a treatment room. Her breathing was labored and erratic. Randy naturally wanted to go into the treatment room with Sue. The ER doctors and staff convinced Randy to wait outside. His emotional state was such that he could impede the ER staff as they endeavored to save Sue. Chief Benson and Mayor Johnson arrived and tried to comfort Randy. Chief Benson spoke to Randy. "Listen, Randy, we're going to get the individual who did this to your wife. I promise you that. State and county officers are assisting us. We will find him!"

Randy looked at the chief and mayor and, in a measured tone, said, "They better find him before I do."

The chief, drawing on 25 years of experience, decided to let Randy handle it in his own way. Randy would have to be monitored to ensure he didn't go off the deep end. He knew that the police, regardless of affiliation, would spare no effort to find the individual responsible. Sue was not a police officer. Nonetheless, she was married to a police officer. That made her "family."

Sue Thompson passed away at midnight. The Westfield General ER staff fought very hard to save her. The ER physician took Randy and Chief Benson into a family room. "Officer," said the doctor, "I am very sorry. We did everything we possibly could to save her. She had just inhaled too much smoke. She fought very, very hard. Again, I am very sorry." The chief comforted Randy, as best he could. The ER staff nurse asked Randy if he would like to see his wife. Randy indicated that he would like a moment alone with his wife.

Sue Thompson looked as though she were sleeping. Folks who perish from smoke inhalation often don't show any outward signs of what killed them. Randy knelt beside Sue's body. He held her hands and told her that he was so sorry. He told her that it was his fault that she died. He castigated himself for not protecting her. Moreover, he could not imagine the horrific last moments of her life. He broke down and cried openly. The mayor and chief backed off in order to allow Randy to grieve. They knew also that he would need time to himself. Randy remained beside Sue's body for another 20 minutes. Mayor Johnson and Chief Benson drove Randy home. They assured Randy that they would be there for him. They asked him if he had family to stay with him. He replied that their families lived back East. He indicated that he would call them with the news. Randy thanked the mayor and police chief. He also thanked the staff sergeant for caring for Nero. He then told the officials that he would be OK. He then added, "I've got Nero, so I won't be alone."

The multiple police agencies looking for Ernie Olsen worked with indefatigable zeal. They were becoming frustrated over their inability to locate Olsen. It seemed as though everything else was frozen in time. The wife of a police officer had been kidnapped and killed. The fact that Sue Thompson perished as a result of an automobile accident did not mitigate Olsen's culpability. He would be charged with kidnapping and vehicular homicide.

Sue's parents and siblings arrived the day after she died. Randy's parents also traveled to Westfield. They stayed at a local motel. They seemed to understand the Nero was supplying the companionship Randy needed. The big dog, so well trained, interacted calmly with the house guests. The guests were stunned by how Nero was so relaxed with them. They, too, had seen police dogs on TV. But spending time with Nero assuaged their depression caused by Sue's murder. They knew that despite the horror of losing Sue, Nero's presence helped Randy cope.

The wake and funeral drew hundreds of police officers from Westfield and surrounding agencies. Randy was overwhelmed by the turnout and genuine concern from everyone. The military and police units are different from civilian organizations. The intrinsic danger attached to those professions brings its members to very strong bonds. Randy felt that he was not alone. His family, his colleagues, and Nero would see him through.

Chapter 16

Ernie Olsen managed to elude the massive manhunt that spread out in all directions following the crash. The police manhunt persisted beyond daybreak. The multi-agency officers were even more dedicated after learning that Susan Thompson had passed away. They knew that the police family had lost one of their own. Ernie had managed to elude the police net by moving through the wooded area in irregular patterns. He surmised that he would have most probably been apprehended if the dog handler joined the hunt. Ernie was no fool; he realized that the cop's wife was either critically injured or dead. He also knew that the police search would only intensify given that a cop's wife was involved. He was right about that!

Randy and Nero returned to duty 10 days after Sue's funeral. Chief Benson had recommended to Randy that he take more time off. Randy thanked the chief, but insisted that work would be therapeutic. The Westfield police officers offered condolences to Randy. He thanked them all. What the rank and file did not understand the closeness that develops between a police or military handler/dog team. Dog handlers compare their affinity to their dogs as comparable to folks' dogs that die after many years as the family pet. Harvey Rhodes related to Randy and his classmates that dog handlers often break down and cry when they kennel their dogs for the last time. Randy had received strong support from his and Sue's family. Nevertheless, Nero was there with him at night. Randy completed his first shift since Sue's death. He sat in his living room with Nero. His home was full of reminders of Sue. He knew that it would take considerable time to overcome his grief. He stroked Nero's head. He thanked his partner. As he prepared to retire for the evening he told his loyal partner, "Don't worry, boy, we are going to find the guy who took Sue from us." Randy did not know how prophetic those words would be.

Most of the Westfield Police Department brass and rank and file thought that Olsen had left the area. They were mistaken. Ernie had waited out the comprehensive search. He survived the initial three days as a fugitive by lying low and stealing food from farmers' fields. He was growing more paranoid by the hour. He decided that he would have to steal a vehicle. He also thought about a home invasion. Ernie knew, however, that he had to split the Westfield area. The cops out here were more organized than he had anticipated. And that damned dog! He told himself that he would kill that fucking dog, given the chance. He knew that he would be caught if he remained in the area. Ernie yearned for the big cities like LA or Detroit. Those cities were much larger than Westfield. It was, told himself, much easier to get lost in those cities.

Randy Thompson continued to grieve over Sue in his own way. He continued to perform his duty. He knew that Westfield citizens were concerned that Olsen was still on the loose. Ladies in particular were nervous; they seldom ventured outside without their husbands. People throughout Westfield offered condolences. Those expressions were heartfelt and meant a lot to Randy. Nevertheless, Randy Thompson knew that his life now had a singular purpose: catch the SOB who took Sue away from him. He would not allow himself to fail. He once again patted his partner gently on his head.

Olsen had decided that he had to split from Westfield. He felt that he had to try to do something about Butch Carter. He realized that eliminating Butch would be next to impossible. The cop world was up in arms over the death of the cop's wife. Olsen had turned back towards Westfield. Ernie told himself previously that it would be next to impossible to get to Carter, but he could not escape the notion that if Carter sang to the cops, his goose was cooked. In reality, he thought to himself, Carter had probably already caved to the cops. He decided that he would find some wheels and leave the area.

Carter had, as Ernie suspected, sang a concerto to the Westfield police. He fingered Ernie within five minutes of sitting down in the interrogation room. Carter surmised that the cops would go easy on him if he cooperated.

That cooperation included ratting out Olsen. The Westfield police called the gang unit in LA. The Los Angeles cops immediately faxed their extensive package on Olsen to Westfield's police. Included in that package was an 8 X 10 glossy of Ernie Olsen. Carter confirmed that, yes, it was a picture of Olsen. Ernie had made it to the outskirts of Westfield. He was unaware that Westfield police officers had his picture.

Randy reported for duty as Ernie was sneaking back into town. He was beginning to trade banter with the guys in the locker room. Police, naturally, like military around the world, lighten the tension by friendly kidding and joking. Cops allow an officer who suffers a loss like Randy had to have as much time as he needed. They wait a period of time until the person signals his willingness to reenter the "locker room" gang. Randy Thompson fully appreciated the respect shown him by his fellow officers. He wasn't quite back all the way. He knew that his fellow officers would have his back. Most of all, he thought, he had Nero!

The handler/dog team hit the road at about 8:30 P.M.. Randy once again immersed himself in his work. He responded to several routine calls. Randy had a much-needed laugh while conducting a routine stop. The two occupants of the vehicle were friendly and cooperative. Randy issued a routine ticket for an expired license. He had the driver sign the ticket and had started to walk back to his cruiser when he was startled by a barking, snarling mixed breed. Randy instinctively jumped back, much to the delight of the occupants of the vehicle. Randy did not see the humor in the situation. He admonished the occupants of the vehicle, informing them that their dog could have bitten him. The driver then made another mistake. "What's the matter, Officer, afraid of old Sam back there?"

Randy smiled and told the driver to stand-by. "I want to show you something." He walked back to his cruiser, gathered up Nero, and walked back to the traffic stop vehicle. When Randy was next to the driver's door, he made a snappy right face with Nero. The driver's eyes nearly jumped out of his face. Randy smiled at the driver, telling him, "It's not nice to scare people with your dog."

Chapter 17

The traffic stop episode brought a smile to Randy. He knew that he would need time to cope with losing Sue. An occasional humorous incident seemed like therapy. He reached for Nero and told his partner, "Good boy, we showed that guy what a real dog looks like."

Randy eased back into a routine patrol when the dispatcher called and asked him to return to headquarters. Randy and Nero walked into headquarters and spotted the shift sergeant approaching.

"Hey Sarge, what's up?" The sergeant handed an 8 X 10 photograph of a male individual to Randy.

"Who's this guy, Sarge?"

"Come into the back office, Randy. I need to talk with you for a moment."

Randy, with Nero in tow, followed the sergeant to an office next to the chief's office.

The shift sergeant showed the photograph to Randy. "This fellow was driving the car that crashed and killed your wife."

Randy stared at the photograph for several minutes without commenting. The shift sergeant could see the intensity in Randy's face. Randy asked the sergeant, his voice choked with anger, "Do we have any idea who this guy is or any information on where he is?"

The shift sergeant told Randy that a massive manhunt had commenced shortly after the accident. He continued, "Every law enforcement agency in the area has been assisting in the search. Don't worry, Ran, we'll get him. I promise you that we will apprehend him."

Randy looked squarely into the sergeant's eyes and said, "Let's hope that someone finds him before I do!" With that, Randy gathered up Nero and walked out to his black and white. He seethed with anger. He headed out to resume his patrol. He knew that he had to keep his wits about himself.

Ernie Olsen had made it back to Westfield without being seen or arrested. He saw an increased police presence throughout Westfield. He knew that he had to steal a vehicle in order to skip town. Ernie managed to keep his cool. He decided that his best chance for pilfering a vehicle would be at a supermarket, box store, or mall. He was working his way towards the heart of Westfield when he spotted an alternate opportunity.

The Pizza Hut delivery truck was parked in front of an upscale high rise apartment building. Ernie eyeballed the pizza delivery truck from between a high rise and a bakery. The young man delivering the pizzas grabbed approximately six pies from the truck. Ernie was not concerned with the small amount of cash the driver had. What he was interested in was the delivery truck. Ernie observed numerous police patrols saturating Westfield looking Sue Thompson's killer. He knew that the police had ramped the manhunt in response to the dead cop's wife.

Ernie timed his move perfectly. He walked up behind the young delivery man as he unlocked his pickup truck. Ernie stuck his Glock pistol into the startled young man's back. Ernie immediately spoke to the young man. "Listen up, son, just do what I tell you to do and you'll be okay."

The young man was terrorized and somehow stammered, "Yes, sir."

Ernie signaled for the young to get into the pickup and slid across to the passenger seat. Ernie warned the young man that he wouldn't hesitate to kill him. The young man nodded to Ernie that he understood. Ernie drove through downtown Westfield, making sure that he did not violate speed limits or any other obvious laws.

Randy was thankful that he had a free run of Westfield. He was driven to find Sue's killer. He would not rest until this animal was apprehended. He had stopped to give Nero a break at a gazebo in downtown Westfield. Nero always attracted attention, whether in the cruiser or taking a break. This evening was no exception. Several families were enjoying the pleasant evening. Randy always kept Nero on leash when citizens were close by. Several young boys and girls approached Randy and Nero. As always, Randy spoke to the folks, explaining all of skills Nero has been trained to perform. Nero performed flawlessly during a short obedience demonstration. A small crowd had gathered at the gazebo. Randy patiently explained how the dogs were trained to accomplish various tasks like attack, building search, etc.

The young pizza delivery man was absolutely mortified. He was a 20-year-old man named Joe Crawford. Joe came from a modest, frugal family. He was working his way through Westfield Community College. Joe had been taught the importance of hard work and self-efficiency. Ironically, Joe was studying Criminal Justice. The young man slumped in his seat. Ernie had threatened to kill Joe if he tried something stupid. Ernie drove the pickup truck towards the south end of Westfield. He surmised that he would home free once he left Westfield.

Ernie was confident that he could evade the Westfield fuzz. He had no reason to suspect that the Westfield cops would look at a pizza delivery truck. Olsen again warned Joe Crawford to keep his trap shut. The Westfield Police Department, with assistance from county officers, had locked down the entire town. Ernie spotted the roadblock a half mile away. He pulled over and parked the pizza delivery truck. He wanted to weigh his options. Ernie slammed his hands on the vehicle steering wheel. He was trying decide how he was going to get out of this fix. His dilemma intensified when Joe Crawford flipped out and tried to force his way out the pizza truck. Olsen grabbed the young man by his collar and strained to pull Joe back.

The young man fought Ernie as best he could. Olsen outweighed Crawford by 20 pounds. The struggle caught the attention of a passing police patrol. The officer backed his cruiser to the pickup. The officer recognized Ernie Olsen right away. He immediately called in to the dispatcher that he had spotted Olsen. Randy Thompson monitored the call from a position in north Westfield. He threw on his lights and sped toward the business district. His adrenaline was rising by the second. He realized that he may soon be face to face with the man responsible for Sue's death.

Ernie Olsen lost his grip of Joe Crawford's collar. Crawford stumbled on the sidewalk after catching his foot on a trash can. That mishap resulted in Joe Crawford losing his life. Ernie was able to scurry out of the pizza truck. He reached for his pistol, a Glock, and shot three rounds into the back of Joe Crawford. The young man with so much to live for died instantly. Ernie took off running into a condominium/apartment building. The responding officer who witnessed the incident ran to the young man lying on the pavement. He once again called dispatch in a much more urgent manner.

Randy Thompson ran code to the scene of the shooting. Nero once again sensed that something big was afoot. He was right. Randy ran over to the officer kneeling over Joe Crawford. He asked the officer where the shooter went. The officer pointed to the condo/apartment complex. Randy looked at the complex. He observed that the building was approximately 15 stories high. He ran to his cruiser and got Nero before heading into the building. Randy and Nero came to a sudden stop after entering the building. What he saw horrified him. Randy and Nero stood above the body of the doorman, who was deceased. He had been shot in the head, point blank.

A phalanx of police descended on the scene. The shift sergeant arrived and took charge of the situation. Several tenants arrived and were quickly hurried away. The sergeant began organizing the operation. "Listen up, guys. This guy is trouble. He's killed two people here and was driving the car that killed Randy Thompson's wife. Keep your head on a swivel." The sergeant assigned officers around the exterior of the building. Randy stood by with Nero, as he had on other occasions. He knew how critical the initial moments were following the crime. Moreover, this case was perhaps not suited for a police dog. Nonetheless, he wanted the sergeant in charge to know he was standing by if needed.

Ernie Olsen had taken the elevator to the highest floor, the 15th. He knew that the fuzz was surrounding the condo/apartment. Olsen stepped out onto the roof of the building to determine if he could escape via another roof. Unfortunately, he determined that the building stood alone. He would have to deal with the cops if he wanted to escape.

The sergeant briefed Chief Benson, who had been monitoring the situation on his police scanner. The murder of two citizens was unprecedented. The chief's cell phone sounded. It was Mayor Johnson asking for an update. Chief Benson told the mayor that he couldn't talk, but would brief him ASAP. For now, he had to get back to the task of capturing Olsen. With the doorman dead, the police had no way to call the occupants to stay inside with their doors locked. The chief decided to dispatch teams of two officers to each floor to inform the residents of the situation.

The officers completed the notifications in 20 minutes. All of the condos and apartments were occupied. This information was good news – so long as Olsen was not already in a unit holding people hostage. Chief Benson and the shift sergeant then assigned teams who would make floor-by-floor searches of the laundry rooms, utility rooms, and anywhere else the fugitive could hide. Randy continued to stand by for an assignment. Chief Benson spotted Randy and Nero and waved him over to he and the shift sergeant. The chief then said, "Randy, tell us how we could use Nero to get this guy?"

Randy replied with enthusiasm, "Chief, police dogs are trained to systematically search buildings for fugitives. Now, we don't usually search buildings as large as this one. What we can do is clear the officers from the building. My guess is that he's hiding in a closet, or perhaps in a false ceiling."

Ernie found what he thought was a perfect hiding place. The condo/apartment was cooled and heated by a nuclear looking plant on the roof. He climbed into a small electric room adjacent to the cooling tower. He held his breath as the cops searched the roof area. He decided that he would wait it out and somehow escape come daybreak. He felt that he didn't have to worry about that damned dog. Once again, the big dog's abilities were underestimated.

Chief Benson called in all of the officers searching for Ernie after 45 minutes. Officers had checked with all tenants of the condo/apartments - all were safe. Olsen had not endeavored to break into a dwelling. Randy was briefed by the chief and shift sergeant. The chief told Randy that he would have 45 minutes. It would just be a matter of waiting out Olsen. The chief told Randy, "Try to flush him out, Randy. These people will be locked in until we get him."

"10-4, Chief, we'll get him!"

Randy Thompson knew that he and Nero had a daunting task ahead of them. He was not looking for glory for himself and Nero. Losing Sue increased his determination to snag this guy. Randy thought back again to training with Harvey Rhodes. Harvey told the class that dogs are easily capable to detect the scent of people one or even two floors above them. "Listen up, guys," Harvey said, "many factors impact a building search with a dog. Remember, when a fugitive hides in a building, his or her scent continues to emanate from their bodies. That scent is subject to gravity and falls toward the ground. Dogs can easily detect a scent drifting from above."

Randy felt very comfortable regarding Nero's ability to pinpoint the location of Ernie Olsen. He realized that this was a most difficult task. He also realized that he could really solidify his standing in the department by bringing this guy to justice. In order to accomplish this, he would have to develop a strategy for searching this massive structure. Randy attempted to, as all cops do, think like the bad guy. His intuition told him that Olsen was hiding near ground level, or near the roof. He decided to search the latter first.

Randy took the elevator to the 14th floor. He did not want to tire Nero, and he certainly could not carry his 90-pound partner up 14 or 15 floors. He took a moment to survey the layout of the building. The layout was typical of most highrise buildings. He saw the usual electric, mechanical, and custodial rooms. He had Nero check those three rooms. They were small enough that Nero would easily detect a person hiding there. Randy had total faith in Nero. He knew that the dog would indicate the presence of a person in those rooms. He then spotted a ladder that led to the roof. The door leading out to the roof was locked. Randy knew that Olsen was not on the roof.

Randy was at the top of stairwell preliminary to descending to the 14th floor when the restroom adjacent to the elevator caught his eyes. Once again, Randy's thought process reverted to Harvey Rhodes' instruction regarding searching buildings. "Remember, guys," said Harvey, "I can assure you that a substantial percentage of people endeavoring to evade police dogs will hide up high. They will frequently hide in false ceilings." Harvey reminded the class once again that human scent is comprised of salt, water, and tiny molecular specs of skin. "Remember, guys," said Harvey, "human scent is subject to gravity."

Randy smiled to himself as he petted Nero prior to entering the restroom. He felt sanguine about the possibility of discovering Ernie in this, or any other restroom. Randy and Nero searched electrical, mechanical and custodial, and restrooms. It happened on the sixth floor. Nero displayed what is called "a change of behavior" immediately after entering the sixth-floor restroom. Randy picked up on Nero's change of behavior right away. The big dog immediately looked up at the eight-foot high false ceiling. Randy reached for his firearm. He was not quick enough.

Olsen pushed aside a false ceiling square and fired three shots at Randy and Nero. Olsen's aim was good; two of the three rounds he discharged struck Randy Thompson. One bullet grazed his left shoulder, while the second hit the left forearm. Neither was life threatening. Randy dived under the row of sinks to his left. It all seemed to happen in a flash. Olsen then lost his balance and fell through the false ceiling. Randy had unholstered his sidearm; he would not have to fire on Olsen. Olsen landed a mere three feet from the handler/dog team.

The Hood chieftain reached for his sidearm. He didn't make it. Nero was on him in an instant.

Numerous emotions ran through his mind. Nero ripped into Olsen's arms and torso. The intensity of Nero's attack on Olsen caused Randy to hesitate. But despite his loathing of Olsen, the dog handler called off the dog with a sharp "Out" command. Out signals to the dog to cease attack. Nero backed off while retaining his interest on Olsen. Randy collected Olsen' firearm. He heaped heavy praise on Nero. Randy was gratified that Nero ceased attack when commanded.

Randy called to the chief and officers, reporting that Olsen had been apprehended. He also told them that he had been shot and Olsen attacked by Nero. It took the shift sergeant, the chief, and a handful of officers two minutes to arrive at the sixth floor. Nero became agitated as the officers entered the restroom. Randy was able to calm down his excited partner. Chief Benson was startled by the sight of one of his officers lying on the floor, having been shot by the other man writhing in pain on the restroom floor. Chief Benson directed that medical help be called post haste.

Randy's injuries looked much worse than they were. Ernie Olsen was not as fortunate. Nero had inflicted serious injury to Olsen. Both of his arms and hands were bleeding, along with his right side. Like Randy's, his injuries were not life threatening. Both were placed on stretchers and taken down the elevators. The shift sergeant read the Miranda Rights to Olsen, who refused to acknowledge his right to remain silent. Nero did not want to leave Randy's side. The EMS crew let Nero ride with them to Westfield General. The sight sergeant felt confident enough to transport Nero to Randy's home. For Randy, this incident was bitter sweet. The satisfaction of apprehending Olsen did not bring Sue back to him. Randy did find poetic justice in witnessing Nero tearing into Olsen.

Randy was treated at Westfield General. He felt fortunate to have basically minor injuries. He knew that it could have been much, much worse. A Westfield black and white unit carried Randy to his home. An anxious, excited Nero went almost berserk with joy when Randy walked through his front door. Randy thanked the officer for the ride. He then settled into his easy chair, a happy Nero at his feet. The house where he had shared so many wonderful moments with Sue now seemed so empty. He wondered how having Nero eased some of his pain. Randy knew that his pain would not ease for some time, if ever. He stroked Nero's head until he fell asleep.

Chapter 18

Randy and Nero had reached rock star status in Westfield. The Westfield Times ran a frontpage story about Nero's latest conquest. Randy responded to the attractive female reporter that all of the credit for this and other exploits should go to Nero. The Times reporter, Carol Moore, put together a concise article which, to Randy's satisfaction, emphasized Nero, and not him. The injuries he had sustained from being shot by Ernie Olsen would not keep Randy from work for an extended period of time. He used this time to deal with personal belongings he and Sue had shared. Randy experienced considerable grief as he rummaged through items he shared with Sue. He became emotional on a number of occasions as he relived special memories they had shared.

The tragedy that took Sue from him was unimaginable. Randy was on the mend and anxious to get back to work. Both Sue's and his families provided as much emotional support as they could. Both families lived out of state. Randy had mixed emotions regarding the two families. He felt that despite their genuine desire to help him, he thought he could recover over time with Nero at his side. Randy spent several days sitting on his patio with Nero. He loved reading about dogs. He was fascinated by the incredible history of people using dogs in so many useful categories from family pets to sophisticated programs like police, narcotic detector, explosive detector, and tracking dogs. The specter of so many other skills and uses solidified Randy's love for Nero. Randy also appreciated how people said that, "Sparky is like a member of the family." While he agreed with and appreciated that statement, he knew that a military or police dog handler probably forms an incredible closeness easily similar to a dog 13 or 14-year pet. Moreover, thought Randy, Nero seemed to understand his master's grief. Randy was an animal lover; his conventional wisdom told him that no other animal comes close to dogs affinity to its owner or vice verse.

Randy was laid up for just two short weeks. The superficial gunshot wounds had completely missed all vital organs or bones. He was once again given a hero's welcome when he returned to duty. Some police officers around the country are jealous or even resentful of canine handlers, as they receive considerable notoriety. The Westfield Police Department was not among those police officers. Randy appreciated the kind words from the chief and mayor. Moreover, the approbation from rank and file officers cemented his position within the force.

Chief Benson, acting on orders from Mayor Johnson, directed Randy Thompson to brief all shifts on Nero's capability's and limitations. Randy was pleased with the reception he received from rank and file officers. He taught the officers that yes, Nero certainly can certainly flush a fugitive out of hiding. He cited the recent incident where Nero took down Ernie Olsen. Randy answered a number of questions asked by fellow officers. He was especially pleased when the various shift sergeants asked questions. Randy never did feel that he and Nero weren't appreciated. Nero's accomplishments had certainly caused city officials to ask why a police dog had not been procured years ago.

Two months had passed since the Ernie Olsen takedown. Randy had just reported to work when he received a call from Westfield reporter Carol Moore. She indicated that the Times was interested in running a story about the handler/dog team.

"Thanks, Carol. I'd have to run it by the brass here. Sounds good. Let me run it by the chief. I'll get back you."

Randy ran Carol's request by the chief, who enthusiastically approved. "Randy," said Chief Benson, "we never want to pass up good publicity."

"Thanks, Chief. I'll do a good job with this reporter."

Randy met with Carol Moore at 10 AM one week later. They met at the Westfield Police headquarters. The police officers and civil servants stared at her as she walked in with Randy and Nero. Carol Moore was a stunning blond, 5' 6", and very well put together. Chief Benson walked out of his office to greet Carol. A brief conversation ensued wherein Carol heaped lavish praise on Randy and Nero. The chief thanked Carol for the positive exposure.

Randy, Nero, and Carol Moore settled into an unoccupied office for the interview that was to lead up to a demonstration of Nero's abilities. Carol interviewed Randy for about one hour. She was amazed at how Nero remained at Randy's side throughout the interview. The Times reporter displayed a genuine interest as Randy explained the working dog concepts. Carol was particularly interested in the history and development of dogs as not only pets but as valuable security and law enforcement partners. With that, they packed up dog and gear and headed out to the Westfield police training facility.

Bob Walsh, the Sommersville PD dog handler, once again came over to Westfield to act as agitator for the demonstration. A dog demonstration always draws a crowd. This "demo" was no different. All police training ceased. The presence of Carol certainly added to the allure. Randy put Nero through the obedience part of the demo. Nero performed his obedience tasks flawlessly, per usual. Randy then explained the controlled aggression sequence to Carol. Most of the police officers had seen Nero in training. Some has seen him in action on the streets. Bob Walsh donned the "sleeve," that he had worn for previous demonstrations. The sleeve, to the dog, is an extension of a man or woman. Harvey Rhodes related a number of examples of dog trainers who had their arms punctured while agitating other dogs. Carol was mesmerized by Nero's power. She was even more amazed at the control Randy had over Nero.

Bob Walsh then hid himself in a two-story building used for training new recruits and SWAT teams. Randy explained to Carol that Walsh was hiding on the second floor. He invited Carol to watch closely as Nero performed a building search. Randy then sat Nero at the lower level door. He then announced loudly, "I have a police dog trained to attack. If you do not come out immediately, I will unleash my dog." Randy then waited for one minute before unleashing Nero. Carol Moore watched with Randy as the big dog commenced searching the building in a systematic manner.

Randy explained to Carol that Bob Walsh had perspired while agitating Nero. He then explained how Bob's scent, comprised of salt, water, and microscopic waste particles, would be like shooting fish in a barrel. Nero had searched one half of the lower floor when he suddenly stopped and looked up. The change of behavior was easy for even an untrained person to see. The big dog then bounded up the stairs in his quest to please Randy. Bob Walsh then jumped out of a closet. Nero launched into full-scale attack. Randy bounded up the stairs prior to calling Nero off the agitator. Carol once again stared in awe as the big dog immediately ceased aggression. Randy thanked Bob Walsh for helping out with the demo. He then jokingly asked Carol if she could mention Bob in the article. Carol shook hands with Bob and promised to mention him in the report. "In fact, Bob," she said, "I'll make sure that a photo of you agitating Nero is included in my report."

With that, she shook hands with Bob, who waved at Randy before heading back to Sommersville.

Chapter 19

The county prison was located 17 miles east of Westfield. Built in 1938, it was one of the oldest prisons in the country. That no one has escaped in over 20 years was a testament to the administration and rank and file prison officers. The county prison was in need of massive upgrade. Lack of funds resulted not only in disrepair. More ominously was a shortage of prison officers; only two-thirds of the authorized slots were filled. Finally, the county prison housed every type of criminal, from petty criminals to rapists and murderers. Unrest among staff and prisoners had spiked dramatically of late. It seemed as though prisoners were likely to detonate at any time. As Randy and Carol Moore were concluding the interview, Chief Benson and the shift sergeant burst into the break room. Randy and Carol could see that something big was up. Carol Moore was about to see Randy and Nero in action. Chief Benson told Randy, "A riot has broken out at the prison. Warden Young has asked for your help. Load up Nero and beat feet to the prison."

Randy replied to the chief's orders with a smart, "10-4, Chief." Carol Moore looked at Randy, who knew what she had in mind.

Randy said to Carol, "Why don't you follow me to the prison?"

Carol was thrilled to be at the center of a real-life situation. She quickly gathered herself and her cameraman.

She wanted to be at the prison when Randy and Nero arrived. Her adrenaline was such that she felt as though she would explode. What she was about to witness would remain fresh in her memory bank for a long, long time.

The unrest at the county prison had been building for several weeks. Warden Victor Young and his subordinates had stepped up all facets of security. Prison scuttlebutt was that a coordinated escape attempt was in the offing. Warden Young had been briefed by his staff gang officers to look for a breakout attempt in the near future. The warden took all of the briefings seriously. Nevertheless, they were becoming routine. This time, the briefings were to come to fruition.

D Block housed the most dangerous criminals. Prison gangs controlled virtually all of D Block. These prison gangs had ties to notorious gangs like the Bloods and Crips in Los Angeles. The Bloods were an offshoot of the more notorious gangs. The apprehension of Ernie Olsen had taken the wind out of the Bloods' standing in and around Westfield. Like all prisons, the gangs were broken into ethnic groups. D Block was comprised of white prisoners. Prisoners of color did not venture near D Block. The same applied to the exercise yard. The D Block corner was located in the northeast corner of the yard. It was there that the D Block gang hatched their plot to escape. On paper, it looked fine. The reality would not only fail; it would devolve into a riot wherein Nero would save a very prominent warden and his secretary.

The D Block gang's plan called for them to start a diversionary disturbance in the exercise yard at noon. D Block leader, Hank Pomeroy, had plotted for weeks a plan to capture the warden and use him as a hostage. Pomeroy was being held at the county jail for distribution of methamphetamine. He had studied the habits of the guards during disturbances and determined that they always came charging ninety to nothing to quell the situation. He had decided that he and his two cronies could make it through the prison with a master key made for them by a jail guard with serious money problems. Pomeroy surmised that he and his two comrades could make it to the warden's office. He knew that he would have to count on other D Block prisoners to create a diversion. Pomeroy promised his D Block comrades that he would do all he could for them through friends in the areas.

At precisely 12 PM, several members of the D Block gang started to verbally harangue adjoining gangs. It took less than one minute for the yard to be engulfed in a full-fledged riot. The alarm horns were blaring, which elicited a spontaneous guard response. Pomeroy and his two confederates drifted towards the entrance to C Block, which led directly to the 2nd floor administration offices, as well as the warden's office.

Randy and Nero, with Carol Moore closely behind, arrived at the prison at 12:45 PM. The commotion in the yard was loud enough for them hear in the parking lot. Randy collected his riot gear and Nero, stopping briefly to tell Carol to standby for now. He emphasized that this was a very dangerous situation. He promised to return and brief her as soon as he could. Randy bounded up the main entrance where the prison guards asked him to standby.

Hank Pomeroy and his confederates, much to their amazement, were able to slip into C Block unnoticed. The conflict outside went on unabated. Hank could not believe their good fortune. The trio had made it up the back stairs undetected. Warden Victor Young and his secretary, Emily Fortune, were alone in the administration complex. The other administration employees had walked to an adjoining catwalk to watch the riot. Pomeroy did not anticipate this stroke of good luck. The three prisoners burst into the warden's office, subduing Emily Fortune. Pomeroy entered the warden's office, taking Victor Young prisoner without resistance. Emily Fortune was bound, gagged, and locked in an office closet.

Carol Moore was growing impatient waiting outside. She approached the main entrance with her cameraman. The guards naturally refused to allow the reporters entrance to the prison. Carol told them that she was a newspaper reporter and a friend of the Westfield police officer who had just arrived.

"Sorry, ma'am," replied the gatekeeper, "those are my orders." Carol was deeply disappointed. She felt as though she would never have a chance for a "scoop" like this one. That sentiment would shift back in her favor in short order.

Pomeroy had been able to contact confederates and arranged a pickup one block from the prison. He had estimated that he and his gang would need approximately 15 to 20 minutes to snag the warden and his secretary. He had instructed them to wait outside of the prison. The driver was to leave at 12:20 PM, sharp.

Hank Pomeroy couldn't control his elation at how smoothly his plan was working. The three thugs bounded the warden and his secretary together. Pomeroy warned the two that they would be stabbed to death if they resisted. The warden seemed stoic, insouciant, while Emily Fortune looked terrified. Pomeroy checked the time. It was already 11 minutes past noon. He realized that they had nine minutes to meet the pickup truck. He had given the outside thugs explicit directions to remain near the front gate until 12:20 sharp!

A convoy of three prisoners and two prison employees departed the warden's office at 12:12 PM. They made it to the top of the rear fire escape stairs without being detected. The prison's captain, Sam Newly, who had been monitoring the riot, wondered why the warden wasn't at his normal observation post along a catwalk.

Captain Newly immediately recognized that things were not as they should be. He drew his Taser and moved down the short hallway to the warden's office. With the door ajar it was easy for him to determine that the warden and secretary were gone. Newly called the main gate to warn the officers that the warden and his secretary were missing. Halt all traffic, in or out! The gates were immediately closed.

Carol Moore had been waiting for what to her seemed like hours. She was naturally curious about how the riot was going. Moreover, she was worried about Randy and Nero. She could tell that most of the noise had abated. That had to be a good sign. She collected herself and told her associate that they have to be ready for anything. It was about to hit the fan!

Captain Newly had organized a "Code Red" alert. Code Red indicated that a possible prison break was underway. Young also informed the prison staff that the warden and his secretary were missing and were likely to have been taken as hostages. The prison policy covering a Code Red upped the intensity of the situation. The county prison had never lost a person. They were not about to lose hostages; that the warden and secretary were captives only intensified the prison guards' efforts.

Hank Pomeroy, his two confederates, Warden Young, and Emily Fortune were hiding in a broom closet located next to the warden's office. Pomeroy knew that it would be difficult, if not impossible to escape the prison without taking the warden and his secretary with them. He thought he had a solution that will give them a chance to get away. He patted down the warden; and wouldn't you know! The warden had a cell phone on his belt. "Thanks, Warden," said Pomeroy. "I hope you have it charged up for me."

The collective force of prison guards and administration personnel quickly ascertained that the fugitives, warden, and Emily Fortune were holed up in the prison administrative area. A search of virtually all of the prison and it's exterior convinced everyone involved in the search that the quartet were hidden within the prison walls. Captain Newly, now in charge of the operation, asked a group of prison guards if any one had checked the administrative complex. Newly directed a number of prison guards to hustle on up and check the area.

Randy Thompson continued to stand by on the first floor. Carol Moore could see Randy and Nero. She knew that he was champing at the bit to help. It was obvious even to a non-security person that this type of operation wasn't exactly conducive to police dog work. She was correct in that assumption. That was, unless the action spilled outside the prison walls. Nero knew, once again, that something big was going down.

Pomeroy checked Warden Young's phone, and sure enough, Captain Newly's prison phone was on the speed dial. Pomeroy asked the warden if the cell phone worked inside the prison.

"Yes," replied Warden Young, "why would we have cell phones that don't work in here?" Young's reply was given in a sarcastic way.

Pomeroy walked over to where the warden and secretary Fortune were sitting in the floor. "Watch your tone with me, Warden. Makes no difference to me if you and your lady there make it out of here!"

Captain Newly's cell phone rang. He immediately recognized the warden's number. Signaling for quiet, he answered, "Yes sir, Captain Newly."

Pomeroy responded to the captain, "Listen, we have the warden and his secretary. If you listen to me, you may see them alive. If you don't do what we say, it's over."

Newly responded, "OK, Pomeroy. What do you want? Rest assured that you are not in a favorable circumstance. Talk to me."

Pomeroy fired back without hesitation. "Listen, cop, I'll be more than happy to. We're going to leave your fine facility with your warden and his secretary. I'll get back to you soon. But let me assure you that the warden and his secretary are goners if you try anything."

Newly and his staff were endeavoring to come up with a plan. They were aware that Pomeroy was doing a 20-year stretch for operating a full-fledged methamphetamine operation in Westfield. The prison staff was well aware of Pomeroy's propensity for violence. Pomeroy had cultivated a reputation as a man better left alone. Newly realized that diplomacy would be called for in order to assure the safety of the warden and secretary.

Randy stood by with Nero, hoping for an opportunity to help bring the standoff to a positive conclusion. He was standing by near the captain when Pomeroy called once again. Newly listened intently as Pomeroy laid out what demands he had for them. Newly put down the cell phone before informing his team that they were demanding a vehicle, $100,000 in cash/unmarked bills, and free passage from the prison. Newly was not told that Pomeroy had arranged for a flight out of Westfield from a small airstrip west of Westfield.

Pomeroy had made significant inroads in Westfield and its surrounding areas in the growing menace - methamphetamine. The city had graduated from a somewhat minor marijuana presence to a burgeoning meth operation. Hank Pomeroy had been in on the growing menace. He was aware that the Westfield Police Department had been occupied with Ernie Olsen, which allowed him to set up shop in Westfield. His operation had been sailing along without a hitch until a raid on his meth lab. The cops had made several buys before closing in on Pomeroy and his minions.

Randy stood by within earshot of Newley's conversation with Pomeroy. His mind was racing at full speed. He was wracking his brain trying to figure out how he could help. Captain Newly instructed his staff to arrange for a car should it come down to that. Randy then asked Captain Newly if he could make a suggestion.

Newly replied, "Sure, Randy, go ahead." Randy suggested that he and Nero could hide in the trunk of the sedan, which could be rigged with a switch that would allow them pop out of the trunk when they arrived at their as yet unknown destination. Newly asked Randy how Nero would react to being in the trunk for a period of time. Randy replied that Nero would be fine as long as they were in there together.

"I'll be able to keep him quiet with a gentle lead muzzle. I'm certain that they won't hear us."

Captain Newly agreed, instructing one of his sergeants to arrange for an unmarked police vehicle with a switch that would allow Randy and Nero to exit quickly. "Tell them to hustle on that assignment."

Pomeroy once again phoned Captain Newly. He cut to the chase, telling Newly that they had one hour to come up with a vehicle and $100,000 cash. Newly responded that it would take time.

Pomeroy cut the captain off. "I don't want to hear any excuses. The mayor's pretty secretary is history in one hour." Pomeroy terminated the call.

Newly turned to his staff. He wanted to know where the hostage negotiator from Sommersville was. One of the sergeants responded to the captain that he should arrive shortly.

"Get his ass in here as soon as he arrives. Has anyone contacted the FBI?"

A sergeant informed Newly that they as well should arrive any moment now. Finally, some good news. Newly was handed a satchel containing $100,000 by a sergeant. The money had been put up by the Westfield Bank. Chief Benson, now on the scene, had guaranteed the money.

The unmarked police car arrived at the prison with five minutes to spare. Captain Newly picked up the phone and called Pomeroy. He then handed the phone to the negotiator. "Inmate Pomeroy, this is Officer McMinn. I'd like to talk you. We have a vehicle at the gate, and we have the money. We want you to help us out by letting the lady go."

Pomeroy's reply was instantaneous. "No fucking way! We will kill your mayor in five minutes unless you tell me the car with the money placed on the hood! And no funny business."

The negotiator relayed Pomeroy's response to Chief Benson and Captain Newly. Chief Benson then told the negotiator to instruct them to come on down.

Randy, with a confused Nero, had been hidden in the trunk. A toggle switch had been installed at the rear of the trunk. Randy was able to assure Nero that it was OK. Carol had watched the handler/team climbed into the trunk. She was even more intrigued by how this situation would play out. She was no longer the lone newshound on site. All three local TV stations were on scene. She felt as though she had a leg up on the TV gang. She was smart enough figure that the prisoners and two hostages were going to come down and leave in the unmarked car. She immediately snatched up the cameraman and ran to their vehicle. She wanted to be in position to follow the car as it left the prison.

Pomeroy again called down to reiterate that Warden Young and secretary Emily Fortune would die at the slightest attempt to intercept them as they depart. "Both of these folks will have sharp knives at their throats. You had better make damned sure that nothing happens." Chief Benson replied that they would not interfere. The chief instructed all officers to stand fast. He had placed two officers with rifles in strategic places. They were instructed to hold off until they received orders to take a shot from the chief and chief only.

Hank Pomeroy, his two soldiers, and the two hostages slowly departed the administration office en route to the stairwell leading to the prison sally port. It was readily apparent that Pomeroy had prepared for the getaway. The warden and secretary, each with a knife at their throats, were positioned in a way that would obviate an opportunity to take out the kidnappers/prisoners. Chief Benson again ordered his sharpshooters to stand down.

The five principles in this drama slowly walked towards the sedan waiting at the main gate. The satchel containing the $100,000 had been placed on the sedan's hood. Prison guards were seething as they stood by helplessly watching the five folks side step to the sedan. Randy continued to reassure Nero as they waited for the scenario to unfold. The dog handler was relieved by the fact that the temperature and humidity were low. Randy thought of Sue and how she would feel about this incident. He was intrigued by Carol Moore. He chastised himself for even thinking of another woman so soon after losing Sue.

Hank Pomeroy drove the sedan. Warden Young was placed in the passenger front passenger seat. Pomeroy made it crystal clear to the warden that any stupid moves would result in Emily Fortune's death. The sedan drove slowly away from the prison. Pomeroy knew that they would be followed. He had made it clear that the hostages would die should the police interfere. Chief Benson had instructed his officers to retain at least a half mile distance from the vehicle. The late arriving FBI agent admitted to himself that the Westfield police handling the situation with aplomb.

Hank Pomeroy had not confided where they were heading until they were situated in the sedan. He knew that few people could keep a secret. He told his confederates that they were heading to a small airplane strip 10 miles north of the prison. When asked how they were going to get away, he told them that a small piper cub airplane would pick them up and fly them away.

"Damn, boss, how did you arrange that?"

Hank replied, "You have to have two things: brains and a reliable partner on the outside. I've got both."

Carol Moore followed at a safe distance. She knew that Randy and Nero were hidden in the sedan's trunk. She was thrilled at the prospect of writing a front-page story on today's activity. She telephoned her editor at the Westfield Times. He was absolutely thrilled to hear about the drama at the prison. He cautioned her to be safe. She promised that she would be safe and get back to him with an update ASAP.

The unmarked car left Westfield in its rearview mirror. The police retained a small presence; they did not want to aggravate Pomeroy and his gang. Carol Moore followed the vehicle at a safe distance. She was surprised by how easy it was to keep track of the sedan without detection. She joked with her cameraman that they should be on a TV police show. Carol's cameraman said "Yeah, I can be Popeye Doyle from the French Connection."

Their disposition changed remarkably as the sedan pulled off the road and drove into a small airport. Circling above was a Piper Cub airplane that could carry up to six people. Hank Pomeroy had coordinated with his contacts. Pomeroy had determined that the three escapees and one of the hostages would fly away. Hank had decided that they would take Emily Fortune with them.

Randy was gratified at how well Nero did during the ride to the airstrip. He could hear the conversation between Pomeroy and his confederates. Their conversation told Randy that they were at an airfield. He knew that they were going to be picked up by a small piper cub. Nero could sense the excitement in Randy's body. The dog handler knew that he could not allow the convicts to depart with one of the hostages. This plan could end up with one or both of the hostages dead.

Carol Moore, watching with her cameraman, saw a small Piper Cub airplane land at the small, remote air field. They watched as the small plane taxied towards the sedan. They were absolutely astonished at what then transpired. The sedan pulled up beside the piper cub, which kept its engine running. Pomeroy emerged from the driver's side door and ordered the two hostages out. Pompey's two confederated followed close behind. The hostages again had knives at their throats. Victor Young and Emily Fortune were pushed towards the piper cub. Carol Moore and the contingent of

Westfield, county, and federal observed from a safe distance. Any overt action by the law enforcement officers would clearly result in the hostages' death. What followed was absolutely astonishing!

The sedan was parked on the tarmac at an angle that allowed Randy to pop the trunk and observe the activities without being seen. Emily Fortune, a knife at her throat, was dragged toward the Piper Cub. She screamed out loud as she and one of the kidnappers approached the Piper Cub. That was Randy's signal to spring into action. He popped the sedan's trunk, which caused Nero to step over Randy. The big dog's leash and chain actually pulled Randy out of the trunk. The scene before him astonished Randy. Hank Pomeroy was busy helping one of his confederates drag Victor Young towards the small side door on the Piper Cub. But Victor Young was not going along with his captors. He managed to momentarily free himself and run away from the Piper Cub.

Pomeroy lit out after Victor Young, who had a 15 to 20-foot lead. Randy Thompson quickly assessed the situation. Nero was wired in on Victor Young and Hank Pomeroy. Randy shouted a command for Pomeroy to halt. The command startled Victor Young and Hank Pomeroy, both of whom stopped in their tracks. The multiple police agencies began to close in. To Carol Moore, what happened next would be imprinted in her memory bank forever.

Hank Pomeroy bolted after Victor Young in an endeavor to regain the upper hand. Pomeroy realized that his only chance was to regain control of the situation. But Pomeroy hadn't realized that Nero was zeroing in on him at 30 miles per hour. Carol Moore watched with awe as Nero caught up with Pomeroy as the thug was about to again confront Victor Young. The warden had frozen in place at hearing Randy's command. Police dogs are trained to respond to movement. Nero hit Hank Pomeroy chest high as the thug raised his knife. The knife went flying as Pomeroy fell onto his back. Randy recovered Nero as quickly as he could, but not before the big dog inflicted significant damage to Pomeroy's chest and arms. Pomeroy's arms were significantly damaged due to his attempts to shield himself, much like a person does when assaulted by a human being.

Pomeroy's two confederates surrendered without incident. The police agencies quickly gained control of the two remaining thugs. Emily Fortune, shell-shocked but OK, was untied and comforted by the Westfield officers. A grateful Warden Young hugged Emily Fortune, both relieved that the ordeal was over. An emergency medical service wagon pulled up on the tarmac. One medic checked Emily Fortune and Victor Young. Two other EMS folks tended to Hank Pomeroy, who required hospitalization. He was charged with a bevy of offenses: prison break, kidnapping, and reckless endangerment.

Carol Moore approached the scene, dazzled by what she had witnessed. She was hoping to have an opportunity to talk to Randy, who was surrounded by a group of police officials. Mayor Johnson and Chief Benson were basking in the glow of Nero's take down. Randy spotted Carol, who was standing on the tarmac at a safe distance. He excused himself and walked with Nero to Carol. He recognized that she was somewhat nervous at being so close to Nero. Randy assured Carol that Nero was fine and she need not worry. She thought that Nero would be fired up so soon after the incident on the tarmac. Randy explained to Carol that dogs like Nero are able to quickly decompress after any incident. "Carol, Nero is like a puppy when not on alert. For example, he can glean from my attitude towards a person that he or she presents a threat." Carol and Randy, along with Nero, walked over to the police officials. Carol wanted to secure a comment from Mayor Johnson or Chief Benson. Randy thanked Carol, who thanked him. They agreed that would get together for coffee or lunch.

PART 2

Chapter 1

Randy and Nero continued to succeed in the battle for control of the war on crime. The elimination of Ernie Olsen and Hank Pomeroy and their ilk had cemented Randy's and Nero's reputation and standing in Westfield. However, like most things in life, nothing remains the same forever. A new menace began to surface in Westfield. Criminals often adapt their operations in any city or metropolitan setting. Such was the case in Westfield. Several months had transpired since the Hank Pomeroy case. Westfield Police detectives had noticed an increase in narcotics in and around Westfield. Cocaine, marijuana, and methamphetamine use had spiked exponentially. Rumors were floating around that the drug pushers had introduced drugs at Westfield high and middle schools. Westfield was not like large cities like New York, L.A., or Houston. The leg work in drug prevention took officers in Westfield away from their assigned duties.

Chief Benson sat down with Mayor Johnson to discuss the growing plague. Johnson read a summary of a report from Westfield General Hospital. The emergency room had experienced a huge spike in drug cases. Moreover, inpatients had also spiked at the hospital.

"Chief, do you have any suggestions?"

Chief Benson didn't hesitate. "Didn't we have this conversation once before?"

The mayor scratched his head before responding, "Are you thinking what I'm thinking?"

The mayor and police chief smiled broadly. The mayor instructed Chief Benson to get the ball rolling. Benson returned to his office. He had Randy check on the cost of Narcotic/Detector Dog training.

Harvey Rhodes smiled as he returned Randy's call. He smiled as he asked Randy, "What took you so long?" Randy recalled Harvey telling him that Southern Training Academy trainers had pretested Nero for narcotic detector dog work. Nero had manifested a keen interest in chasing rubber balls and play towels us as a reward for locating narcotics or explosives. Randy then briefed Harvey on his success at taking out the like Olsen and Pomeroy.

Explosive and Narcotic Detector Dogs are very expensive. The price of a Narcotic Detector runs in the neighbor of $15,000 dollars. That price includes the dog as well as the training. Westfield would pay for the training, in the area of $10,000, to have Nero trained to sniff out drugs. Randy briefed the chief, who then briefed Mayor Johnson. The mayor did not hesitate to instruct Chief Benson to get the ball rolling.

Randy and Nero were on their way to Southern Training Academy 10 days after the mayor blessed the project. Things had been happening to Randy at a mind splitting pace. His work with Nero over the preceding year and one half had been unbelievable. The death of his wife Sue was extremely painful. Randy knew that his work with Nero helped lessen the pain. He relived with considerable pain every aspect of the circumstances surrounding her death. He pledged to continue on with making Westfield safe. Every positive outcome was dedicated to Sue. In his mind that would never change.

Harvey Rhodes met Randy and Nero at the airport. The veteran dog trainer was genuinely pleased to see Randy and Nero. Harvey offered heart felt condolences to Randy regarding the tragic loss of Sue Thompson. Randy thanked his instructor, who could see the dog handler tear up. Harvey let a moment pass before patting Randy on his shoulder. Randy thanked Harvey for his concern. The remainder of the drive to Southern Training Academy was filled with small talk, with Randy briefing Rhodes about Nero's stellar work. As they pulled up to the raucous sound of barking dogs, Randy looked at Nero and said, "I don't know how I would have held myself together without my partner." Harvey just smiled, fully aware of the impact a police dog has on its handler.

The Narcotic Detector Dog course would run four weeks. A total of six handler/dog teams would train with Harvey Rhodes. The other five teams, like Randy, were experienced dog teams, graduates of Southern Training

Academy. Harvey explained that the fact they already had a leg up would be most beneficial to the class.

"You will find that your understanding of your dogs' habits and mannerism's will assist you in training your dog to search for drugs."

Randy was once again enthralled by the prospect of advancing his understanding of how these magnificent animals operate.

Chapter 2

Harvey Rhodes convened the class at 8 AM on the morning following. He could see the enthusiasm in the dog handlers' eyes. "Good morning, lady and gentlemen," said Harvey.

This class consisted of five male and one female officer. Rhodes had trained all six handlers as rookies in the canine realm. Moreover, Harvey had pretested all six dogs for their suitability as Narcotic Detector Dogs. Harvey then had each officer stand up brief the class on how they had fared in their respective cities. Several related successful inaugurations in their respective cities. None of his classmates came close to matching Randy and Nero's record. All six of the handler/dog teams had impacted their respective cities crime waves. All six worked in cities like Westfield where they represented the initial canine teams.

Harvey then informed the class that the initial day, much like police training would be dedicated to laying a foundation of understanding what to expect in the coming weeks. Harvey then launched into a four-hour lecture on the history and development of Narcotic Detector dogs. Randy and his classmates were once again enthralled with the information presented by Harvey.

"Basically, what we do is teach the dog to associate the odor to a reward." Harvey continued, "You will be amazed at a dog's ability to pinpoint the location of illicit drugs and drug paraphernalia. And you guys have the advantage of understanding your dogs' habits and particularities." Randy's mind was racing ninety to nothing.

Harvey then presented a detailed sketch of utilizing dogs for drug or explosive detection. Harvey explained the basic concept. "What we do is really very fundamental: we teach the dogs to associate the odor of illegal drugs to the reward. Some dogs like to play with hard rubber balls, while some dogs prefer a towel or a larger hard rubber toy." Harvey hesitated long enough to observe his students. Their undivided attention told Harvey that this would be a superior class.

Harvey spent the remainder of the day explaining the fundamental concept of detector fog use. "We start off with what we call basic retrieve. Basic retrieve involves introducing your dog to marijuana. You will show the narcotic, then toss it just a few yards, clearly in view of the dog. You will then show the dog the ball/towel and encourage your dog to 'seek', in a very enthusiast voice. Guide the dog to the narcotic. When the dog puts its nose on the narcotic, praise him lavishly and give him the ball or towel. It is essential that you demonstrate a very enthusiastic tone." Harvey was pleased to see the intensity on the students' faces.

Harvey concluded the initial day by showing a video of various agencies conducting actual drug raids with narcotic detector dogs. Randy and his classmates were enthralled by the dogs' astonishing ability to locate illegal drugs hidden in automobiles, luggage, offices, and in open fields. Randy and his classmates could not wait to start training with their dogs. Harvey concluded the day by reminding the class that what they witnessed were handlers with extensive experience.

"Remember," said Harvey, "that you will have to approach this training in a sensible manner. You all are familiar with your dogs. I am looking forward to working with all of you."

Chapter 3

Randy's class did not need a handler/dog orientation period. Harvey said that they would be moving into introducing their dogs to the narcotics and reward program in short order. Rhodes had the class repair to the training room. He then introduced the class to some terms that would become second nature to them. The instructor then spent about one hour teaching the class terms like threshold, seek, extinction, reward schedules, successive approximation, and cornering. Harvey explained to the class that the threshold is the exact place where the search commences, like at the doorway into an office or warehouse. The term "seek" is the command that commences the search. The term "extinction" refers to the practice of eliminating unwanted behavior by not overreacting to reasonable problems in training. Reward schedules are used to teach the dog to complete searches prior to receiving a reward. Cornering is a technique where a dog working an office, for example, is taught to check the corners of a room in the hope of picking up the scent of illegal narcotics that have accumulated in a corner.

Harvey explained to the class that those terms all have an impact on how proficient the dog can become in the hunt for narcotics. "Don't worry, guys, it will all come together. I'm sure that you all will do very well. I'm actually pretty good at this game. Let's go outside. We're going to watch a demonstration of a trained Narcotic Detector dog perform a search for marijuana. This exercise is presented in a format referred to as 'whole-part-whole.'"

Harvey introduced Jackie Hutchinson, one of his assistant trainers, and his trained narcotic detector dog, Sampson. "Let's watch Sampson at work. I'll break it down after the demo."

The Southern Training Academy staff had placed eight suitcases in a line. Harvey explained that one of the suitcases contained a bag with one hundred grams of marijuana.

"Watch how Sampson works the suit cases. This is a very basic test for Sampson." Harvey signaled Jackie Hutchinson to begin.

Hutchinson and Sampson approached the row of suitcases. The class watched closely as Hutchinson reached the first suitcase. The handler hesitated, retrieved a hard rubber ball from a pouch on his work belt. Jackie then returned ball to the pouch and pointed to the first suitcase while enthusiastically telling Sampson "seek." Sampson began sniffing the suitcases in a systematic, thorough manner. The students were amazed at how the dog did not need any guidance after being commanded to "seek" by his handler. Sampson's energy level seemed to increase as he approached the final two or three suitcases. Sampson arrived at the penultimate suitcase, where he immediately intensified his interest by scratching the suit case. Hutchinson took the hard rubber ball and bounced it while telling Sampson, "Good boy, Sampson, you found it. Good boy!" Jackie opened the seventh suitcase. He then held up a plastic containing fifty grams of marijuana.

The class watched as Hutchinson gathered up the ball from Sampson and guided the dog to the final suitcase. Sampson searched the final suitcase without responding. Hutchinson heaped heavy praise on Sampson for a job well done. He did not reward the dog with ball at the conclusion of the exercise. Only one of the six novice drug dog handlers picked up on the fact that Sampson did not get to play with the ball. The novice was Randy Thompson.

Harvey thanked Hutchinson and Sampson before turning to the class. Rhodes could see the enthusiasm in the in the faces of the class. "What do you all think about Sampson?" Harvey then went on, "What you saw there was a very experienced team. Jackie and Sampson have been teamed up for four years. What you saw was a trial that did not challenge Sampson. Jackie was a student just like you all about four and one half years ago."

Harvey then explained that the first exercise is called "basic retrieve." He told the class that they were to toss a bag containing fifty grams of marijuana about ten feet. They were then show the ball to the dog before encouraging it to "seek" in a very excited voice." Harvey then instructed the handlers to lead the dogs to the bag of Marijuana. They were told to take the rubber ball out of the pouch and bounce it very enthusiastically while praising the dog verbally. Randy and his classmates were pleased at how the dogs easily connected the odor of the drug to the ball.

Harvey then explained to the class that many folks thought that narcotic detector dogs develop a liking to the drugs. Rhodes then explained the reality. "Folks, narcotic detector dogs don't give a hoot and a holler about marijuana, cocaine, heroin, meth. To the dogs it is a way to get to play with the ball."

Harvey then had each handler perform a basic retrieve with his/her dog. All of the dogs did well; none, however, did as well as Nero.

The instructor had the handlers perform a series of basic retrieve exercises. Jackie Hutchinson observed and corrected a few of the minor flaws. The remainder of the day was dedicated to basic retrieve. Randy Thompson could hardly contain himself. His fellow students exhibited similar enthusiasm. The class gathered for dinner that evening. They shared their respective experiences with their dogs. None of his classmates' experiences came close to matching his.

The following days were filled with a gradual uptick in difficulty. From basic retrieving, they moved to suitcases, desk drawers, vehicles, and open areas. Jackie Hutchinson made it a point to explain a very important principle peculiar to narcotic detector dog training.

"Class," said Jackie," we have been gradually increasing the difficulty of your exercises. From basic retrieving, we have had the dogs' search suit cases, desks with their drawers open. We refer to this principle as 'successive approximation' or 'shaping.'"

Randy and his classmates were once again mesmerized by the information presented by Jackie Hutchinson.

Jackie continued, "A simpler explanation would be simple to complex. We want the initial trials to be easy for both dogs and handlers. Rest assured that the trials will become more challenging. Let me explain something to you. The key to a successful drug detector lies with the handler. Dogs do not have bad days. Unless your dog is sick or injured he will perform for you. It's up to the handler to set an enthusiastic persona every day!"

True to Jackie Hutchinson's word, the trials became more difficult. Suitcases were now closed, desk drawers were now closed, and automobile trunks were now closed. The instructors continued introduce more and more trials. Marijuana was hidden in false ceilings. Handlers were taught a very fundamental principle: look where the dog looks! Like human scent, narcotics are organic, thus its odor are subject to gravity. Nero was clearly the most proficient dog in this class.

Harvey Rhodes and Jackie Hutchinson introduced the class to what are referred to as "hard" drugs.

"Heroin, cocaine, methamphetamine, and hashish are what we see on the streets of America," Harvey explained in detail the difference in searching for marijuana versus hard drugs.

Rhodes continued, "Marijuana has a much more pungent odor than hard drugs. Dogs must get closer to the drug or 'source' when searching a car, office, etc."

The handler/dog teams were developing confidence in their dogs' ability. True to Harvey's words, the class found detecting hard drugs more difficult. Nevertheless, they found it very stimulating and rewarding. The class as a whole was doing very well. The instructors were pleased with the progress.

The intensity of the training accelerated as the class rapidly approached the conclusion of the four-week training. Randy and Nero worked perfectly together. His success rate with Nero was 98 percent, top in the class.

Harvey Rhodes and Jackie Hutchinson worked very hard at imparting as much information they could. They wanted the students prepared for what was ahead. Jackie spoke to the class on a very critical topic: legal matters. Instructor Hutchinson explained as best he could that narcotic detector dogs are used to locate illicit drugs, as well, and equally important is the establishment of Probable Cause.

Jackie continued, "Make sure that you check in with your district attorney. In fact, we recommend that you and your chief, mayor, and district attorney get together to establish a protocol for their respective cities or counties."

Graduation day finally arrived. The class members were anxious to get back home and commence fighting the narcotic problems in their cities. Randy had taken stock on all that he and Nero had learned. He knew that he would be under scrutiny when he began to combat the drug trade running rampant in Westfield. Together, he and Nero had learned so much! Randy had supreme confidence in Nero's ability. He saw no reason to expect anything less. The key, he told himself, was to approach this new challenge like he did with Nero two years ago. Randy thanked Harvey and Jackie and promised to keep in touch.

Chapter 4

Randy arrived back to Westfield at 7:30 on a Friday night. Benson and a shift sergeant met Randy and Nero at the small Westfield airstrip. Randy explained that the last leg of the trip was kind of rough. He and Nero were glad to be able to stretch their legs. Chief Benson greeted Randy, shaking hands, and petting Nero. The big dog was familiar with the chief. "Welcome home, Randy, we're really glad to see you. How did it go down there?"

Randy told the chief that he was sure glad to be back home. Nero even seemed more relaxed after seeing some familiar faces. Randy and Nero rode in the back seat of the chief's cruiser. The chief was anxious to hear how Nero had done. The proud dog handler handed a certificate the shift sergeant. The sergeant looked it over, smiling as he told Chief Benson that Randy and Nero were the honor graduates for their class. The chief gave an "atta boy" to Randy.

The chief then began to catch Randy up on the happenings in Westfield over the preceding month. "Well, Randy, it's like this: people who fought for our country said that every time they'd take out a Viet Cong, two more would take his place. That's pretty much what happened here. We, well, you and Nero put Ernie Olson and Hank Pomery out of commission. And as so often happens, we now have a couple of new thugs taking over."

The chief hesitated before continuing. "The fundamental difference this time is that drugs are their single concern."

The shift sergeant followed up the chief's remarks by telling Randy, "It's even showing up in middle and high schools. We haven't had much of an uptick in violent crime. But you can rest assured that it's coming."

The chief dropped of Randy at his home. Chief Benson told Randy to get some rest. "Why don't you come in tomorrow at 10 AM? We have a number of folks who are anxious to see you and meet Nero."

Randy still felt pangs of hurt and loneliness each time he entered his and Sue's home. They say that time heals hurt or losses. He realized that it would take more time, if ever to get over it. Nero seemed to sense Randy's melancholy. The big dog lay down next to Randy, actually making contact. Randy hugged Nero firmly. He just sat there holding Nero, tears in his eyes. "You're right, buddy, she was something special."

Randy strolled smartly into the Westfield Police Department at 10 AM the following morning, Nero proudly by his side. Mayor Johnson, Chief Benson, and a host of police brass and employees were present. The mayor approached the handler/dog team. Mayor Johnson stopped two paces from the team.

"Welcome back, Randy, we have been anxiously awaiting your return. I know that the chief briefed you last night. We have a lot of work for you."

Randy replied to the mayor, "Thanks, Mayor. Nero and I are ready to tackle the drug problem." Randy continued to glad hand the visitors, many of whom wanted to take pictures of the team with their phones.

Mayor Johnson surprised the gathering by informing them that Randy and Nero would be giving them a demonstration of Nero's new skill. Randy gave the gathering a brief rundown of what they were going to see. Randy asked the assembled crowd to look at the parking lot behind the building. He had arranged for six suitcases in a row. One of the suitcases contained a bag which held 50 grams of marijuana. The weed was hidden in the fifth case. Randy warmed up Nero by showing him the ball. Randy then led Nero to the first suitcase, telling him "seek." The big dog systematically searched from left to right, sniffing each suitcase. The observers were captivated by the manner in which Nero searched the suitcases. Nero's response to the fifth suitcase enabled the uninformed to see that Nero had responded to something in that suit case. Randy rewarded Nero by bouncing the ball and telling Nero "Good boy, that's the way to go."

Randy allowed Nero to play with the ball for a few seconds. He then gathered Nero, put the ball in its bag before having Nero search the final bag. Randy brought Nero back inside to a round of applause. He then asked the folks to look outside at the suitcases. A Westfield officer proceeded to open each suitcase. When the officer opened the fifth suitcase a bag holding 50 grams of marijuana fell to the floor. Randy then answered a number of questions from a very appreciative audience.

Carol Moore was present, along with two TV teams. She had remained in the background for the majority of the meet and greet. She approached Randy and Nero after the crowd dissipated. Randy smiled as Carol approached.

"Welcome back, Randy," she said. "How was drug dog school?"

Randy joked with Carol, telling her, "It is called Narcotic Detector Dog school, ma'am." Nero wagged his tail as he recognized Carol. They visited for several minutes before agreeing to get together soon for coffee.

Randy and Nero went back to work after resting for two additional days. Westfield detectives briefed Randy about the increasing menace caused by narcotics. The chief had developed a protocol for Nero's entry into service. Chief Benson wanted officers to call for the dog if they even suspect that illicit drugs are present during all traffic stops. Randy was once again gratified by the interest the detectives displayed. All indications were that Nero would have an immediate impact on the drug program. It would not take Randy and Nero to pay dividends.

Randy retained his 8 pm – 4 am shift. Nero was eager to hit the road. Patrolling the streets again stimulated Randy as well. Randy was again amused by how Nero managed to turn heads. The early hours of his patrol were routine. A call from a unit on the West side of town snapped Randy into action. A Westfield unit had pulled over a sedan for a burned-out tail light. The occupants seemed overly nervous about such a routine infraction. Both officers smelled what they thought was Marijuana. Police officers across the country have been exposed to burning Marijuana. Harvey Rhodes had related an incident wherein a United States Air Force Narcotic Detector dog handler testified that burning Marijuana smelled like "burning rope." The military judge threw out the case, declaring, "Burning rope is burning rope – burning marijuana is burning marijuana! Case dismissed."

Randy pulled up behind the unit that had pulled over the sedan. The occupants were standing in front of the police cruiser. The officers informed Randy that they thought they smelled burning marijuana in the sedan. They had patted down the two occupants; they were clean. Randy asked the two men if they would grant the police permission to search the vehicle – they declined. Randy then informed them that these officers had smelled what to them was burning marijuana. The demeanor of the two men changed when Randy went to his cruiser to retrieve Nero.

Randy hesitated briefly to check the wind direction. He reflected on training with Harvey Rhodes and Jackie Hutchinson. Harvey told the class to always approach a vehicle from the "downwind" side. The downwind side is basically the "bottom" of the wind direction.

Jackie broke it down for us. "If you are going to search a vehicle, you would check the wind by wetting a finger and holding it up. You will be able to feel the wind direction. For example, if the vehicle were parked facing north, you would commence your search at the rear, or 'downward flank.'"

Jackie then explained that you would assist the dog by gently tapping on the door, trunk, and engine compartment seams. Jackie emphasized to the class to always search into the wind. This method would give the dog the advantage of having the odor of the narcotic flowing toward the dog.

Randy approached the sedan from the rear as it was parked facing north. He was confident yet somewhat nervous as this was his first real search with Nero. Nero started a systematic search of the vehicle following an enthusiastic "seek" command from Randy. The two officers, as well as the two occupants, watched as Nero sniffed the trunk, the wheel and wheel wells, passenger and passenger doors. Narcotic Detector dogs are taught to search left to right, regardless of the item or area to be searched. This method established a familiarization for the dogs, which cut down the chances of overlooking illicit narcotics.

Nero had searched the trunk area, as well as the right side of the vehicle. The dog manifested a very noticeable change in his behavior as he sniffed the front passenger door. Nero immediately scratched the passenger door. Randy encouraged the dog, telling him, "Good boy, Nero, good job" while bouncing the rubber ball. Randy regrouped Nero before waiving to the officers. "Fellows, my dog has responded to the presence of illegal narcotics. Please read their rights to the occupants of this vehicle."

Randy proceeded to search the sedan. He unsnapped Nero who bounded into the front seat of the sedan. The big dog immediately scratched vigorously at the glove compartment. Randy popped open the glove compartment. Nero was becoming unglued as Randy grabbed a large plastic bag containing 200 grams of marijuana. Randy once again bounced the ball for a deliriously happy Nero. Randy was just ecstatic over Nero's performance. He briefed the sight sergeant, who had arrived at the exact moment Nero was pawing the glove box.

The two patrol officers made a point to indicate to the shift sergeant how well Nero had performed. Randy could not have asked for more. The handler/dog team had gotten off to a fabulous start. Randy smiled to himself. This incident was not even a reasonable challenge for Nero. Randy was smiling because his fellow officers had no clue regarding the difficulty of the search. All they saw was Nero responding to a vehicle with illicit drugs hidden in the glove box. And to boot, the shift sergeant was present for most of the bust.

Word of Nero's success shot through the on-duty officers. Randy returned to headquarters to accomplish an incident report for the bust. Officers applauded and barked at Randy when he and Nero walked in to the desk sergeant desk. Randy appreciated the recognition, particularly the barking. It indicated that the rank and file were pulling for them. Nero just sat beside Randy, nonplussed by the humans barking at him. The remainder of their first night passed without serious incident. Randy could not have scripted a better beginning.

Chapter 5

Westfield, like most cities, was experiencing rapid growth. Westfield was not plagued by the open violence found in Chicago or Oakland. Nonetheless, Mayor Johnson and Chief Benson were receiving reports of increased narcotic activities in Westfield. The movers and shakers of the drug traffic were accustomed to moving their product with impunity. The Westfield Police Department had been occupied shutting down Ernie Olsen and Hank Pomeroy and their minions. The Westfield School had received alarming reports of increased narcotic activity on high school as well all way down to middle schools.

The Superintendent of the Westfield Independent School District called the chief to ask for help with the influx of drugs at the high schools and middle schools. Chief Benson and Superintendent Fred Robinson had been friends for years. Robinson was a lifetime resident of Westfield. He preceded Chief Benson by one year at Westfield High School. The chief told Fred Robinson that his timing could not be better.

"Fred, this could not have come at more fortuitous time. You must have heard that one of our officers, Randy Thompson, recently returned to Westfield with a narcotic detector dog. He took down a couple of guys with a bunch of marijuana on his first night out with the dog."

Fred then asked Chief Benson if it was possible to have Randy and Nero visit a couple of schools during assemblies.

"Fred," replied the chief, "I'm sure that Randy would be thrilled to visit. Just let us know when."

Randy was ecstatic at hearing the news. "You betcha, Chief. Glad to do it. I think we can contribute to the community by educating our young people about the danger posed by drugs."

It was a quiet, serene Saturday night. Serene as it could be for the first three hours of patrol for Randy and Nero, anyway. They had responded to several routine calls involving traffic stops, noise complaints, etc. That all changed just a few minutes before midnight. It all started with a routine call to a west side patrol regarding a family disturbance. Any police officer will tell that domestics are hands down one of the most dangerous calls that police respond to. Randy headed to the incident address with Nero riding high in the passenger seat, his huge head sticking out of the window.

Nero displayed a heightened awareness as they approached the scene of the disturbance. Randy would swear to himself that Nero could tell when something was about to go down. This incident would cement that impression regarding Nero. Numerous police vehicles, lights flashing, lined the street of the incident. Per usual, Randy parked behind several black and whites. He gathered Nero and quietly walked up to an officer, who told Randy that two men had invaded the home of a family of five and were holed up on the second floor of the home. Randy asked the officer if he had any additional information on the family or invaders. The officer said that he had heard rumors that the man of the house was a big-time businessman. That's all the young officer knew.

The family of Derrick Brewster resided at 817 Olney Avenue. Derrick's wife Audrey and he had three children and had been married for 18 years. Derrick Brewster was president of Brewster's Home and Auto Insurance Service. Derrick had worked his way up the corporate ladder under the tutelage of his father, Wesley Brewster. Derrick had taken control of the business when Wesley Brewster dropped dead of a heart attack. Wesley Brewster was still warm in his grave when Derrick began implementing sweeping changes. He had been encouraging his late father to modernize Brewster Insurance. The senior Brewster was "old school." He did not see the need for all of these newfangled computers. He continued, until his sudden death, to believe that face-to-face contact trumped the modern way.

Derrick Brewster invested thousands of dollars into the business. Problem was, he managed to run a hitherto solvent company down a path to certain failure. Derrick did not handle pressure. He turned to drugs to help him cope. Derrick's secretary, Daisy Gonzalez, knew that large amounts of cash were being siphoned from the company coffers. Daisy had worked for Brewster Insurance for 20 years and was not about to jeopardize her standing with the agency. The reality was that the missing money was going right up Derrick Brewster's nose.

The pressure of running his insurance company, keeping his wife Audrey, who seldom passed up an opportunity to shop happy, and a dramatic drop in sales had taken their toll on Derrick Brewster. Derrick was cruising around Westfield's East Side on a rainy Wednesday evening. He was in no hurry to get home and listen to Audrey's bullshit about not being able to shop seven days per week. Derrick had tried marijuana in college. That was just for kicks. He needed something a bit stronger! He eyed two men leaning against a convenience store. They eyed him back and recognized him for what he was: a well-to-do, upward, mobile white guy looking for a hit.

Derrick pulled his Volvo into the store parking lot and waited for the two men to approach. They didn't mince words. "What ya looking for, man?"

The two men recognized that this was no cop. Derrick tried to conceal his anxiety. He spoke, his voice trembling. "What have you got that can help me through a tough time?"

One of the two men leaned into the Volvo and told Derrick that he had to great cocaine. The deal was done in less than one minute. Derrick returned to his now empty insurance agency. He sat at his desk staring at the small baggie of cocaine. He had read stories about coke. He had seen news stories on TV about how addictive it can become.

Derrick's life changed instantly. The euphoria he felt was unlike any sensation he had ever experienced. Snorting the white powder seemed to make everything all right. It took a few short weeks for Derrick Brewster to become a full-fledged junkie. The two pushers were making almost daily deliveries to Derrick. He would call them to arrange a meeting at a McDonald's one block from his agency. Daisy Gonzalez' intuition told her that her boss was a junkie. She had promised herself that she would confront him about it. She never did.

The police response to 817 Olney Avenue was precipitated by a hostage situation. The two junkies who had reeled in Derrick Brewster had allowed him to run up a sizable tab. They were under the mistaken impression the Brewster was wealthy. He had told them that his shortage of cash was temporary. They believed him. However, when it became obvious that he was ignoring them, they acted.

At 10:30 PM that Saturday night, the two thugs strong-armed their way into the Brewster home. Audrey was reading in the living room. Their three children were fast asleep upstairs. Derrick Brewster had emerged from the shower when he heard a commotion downstairs. He threw on a robe and ran downstairs to see what caused the noise. Derrick was astonished to see the two men who had been supplying him with coke were standing in his living room. All of the color left his face as he realized what he saw unfolding in his home.

The two street thugs did not hesitate to inform Audrey that his husband owed them $15,000 for his unpaid cocaine tab. Audrey heard the children stirring. The invaders told her to stand fast. She looked at her husband, a bewildered look on her face. The thugs ordered the entire family upstairs. They cut to the chase.

"Derrick," said one of the thugs, "you are going to go to your company to get $15,000 in cash. You have one hour. If you aren't back, say goodbye to these folks. And if we see even one cop, they're dead! You've got one hour."

Chapter 6

Derrick Brewster stumbled to his Volvo, wondering how he could have put his family in such jeopardy. He did his best to keep his wits about him. He could barely fit his key into the ignition. Once underway, he experienced increased anxiety. He chastised himself for not telling the thugs that his company did not keep large sums of cash in his office. The multifarious pressures were too much for Derrick. He was driving in such an erratic manner that he was pulled over less than one mile from his home. The patrol officer approached the vehicle as he had done on countless occasions. What he saw was a man who looked as though he was coming apart at the seams.

Derrick Brewster was able to convey to the officer why he was driving in such an erratic manner. The patrol officer immediately contacted dispatch. The officer related to dispatch that the thugs had threatened his family if they saw any police. The shift sergeant directed that police were to remain a minimum of two city blocks from the Brewster residence. The patrol officer drove Derrick to the Westfield Police headquarters. The shift sergeant asked Brewster to brief him in detail about what was going down at 871 Olney Avenue. He did so, omitting the part about his cocaine addiction.

The shift sergeant realized that he was in a dicey situation. Two thugs had a woman and her three children hostage in their own home. Their husband was sitting before then at police headquarters, looking as though he was about to cry. The shift sergeant instructed the desk sergeant to call Chief Benson and appraise him of the situation. The chief instructed the shift sergeant to respond in force to 871 Olney Avenue. Benson told the dispatcher,

"We have no chance to save those people if we stay away. I'll be at the scene in 10 minutes."

Audrey hugged her children as she tried to calm them. She was terrified herself. Her world was crashing down fast. Not only were she and her children held hostage by two thugs, but she also had confirmed what she thought for months: Her husband was a certified junkie! Audrey had been married to Derrick for 18 years. She thought that she knew him. The reality, she thought, was exactly what folks frequently said: "You never really know anyone!"

Chief Benson ordered a full-fledged response to 871 Olney. A command post was established in the street in front of the Brewster home. Elmer Benson knew that he was taking a chance, but his heart told him that if he didn't, this situation could end tragically. He trusted his gut instinct. That was the scene Randy saw upon arriving at the Brewster residence. Randy thanked the young patrol officer he spoke to when he arrived at 871 Olney Avenue. Randy caught Chief Benson and the shift sergeant's eyes. They waved back at him. He wanted them to know he was there if needed.

The shift sergeant moved close to the Brewster home where he addressed the individuals inside with a loud holler: "This is the Westfield Police. We have the house surrounded. We know that you have Mrs. Brewster and her children. You must come out now!"

Chief Benson spoke to the shift sergeant, "Any suggestions, Sarge?"

The sergeant said, "Not right off the top of my head, Chief."

Randy, with Nero in tow, inched closer to the chief and his entourage. He realized that this would be a tricky situation that may not be suited for a police dog. Westfield would soon learn of the versatility of Nero. They wouldn't have to wait long.

Audrey Brewster huddled with her three children in the master bedroom. One of the drug pushers was watching Audrey and the children. The other was eyeballing the scene outside one of the kids' room. He then returned to the master bedroom to inform his partner of the cop's presence. The pusher guarding the woman and kids said, "Great, now what the fuck are we going to do?"

His partner replied, "We'll come up with something. We're in the driver's seat as long as we have the woman and kids. Let me think!"

The chief told the shift sergeant to try the loud bullhorn again. Once again, no response. Derrick Brewster had provided a sketch of his home. The chief was in the middle of talking to his officers when he was interrupted by a shout from a window on the second floor of the Brewster home. One of the two thugs shouted to the police contingent gathered around the Brewster home. "Listen up, cops, we have the woman and her three kids! You had better back off. This will not end well."

Chief Benson looked at the shift sergeant. They both seemed to hit on the same notion. The shift sergeant said what they both thought, "If one is yelling out a window, the other has to be watching the woman and kids. Chief, we have to get a man inside."

Randy Thompson heard the conversation between the chief and shift sergeant. His mind was racing, looking to find a way for him and Nero to rescue the family held by the two junkies. Randy took a deep breath as he gathered himself before offering a suggestion.

"Excuse me, Chief," he said, "can I offer a suggestion?"

Chief Benson replied, "Go ahead, Randy, what do you have?"

Randy responded, hoping that he was not out of line, "Chief, with just two men up there, I could take Nero around back. I'm sure I can break in quietly with Nero."

The chief and shift sergeant exchanged quizzical looks. Chief Benson replied, "I don't recall ever hearing of a police dog team entering a home with hostages inside. Isn't that a bit risky?"

Randy didn't hesitate before replying, "He'll be on leash, Chief. We all know how the thugs freak out at the very sight of a trained police dog."

Chief Benson responded, "Let me dwell on that, Randy. Stand by."

The situation quickly tilted towards Randy's suggestion. The thug apparently in charge reappeared at the hallway window. "Listen up, cops, I'm going to tell you just one time: I want a car parked in front of this house within five minutes. If it's not here, we'll throw the body of one of the kids out this window." That said, he slammed down the window and disappeared from view.

Chief Benson could not recall a more pressure-packed incident. He had to react, fast. Tear gas was out of the question with the mother and three children inside. He turned to Randy and said, "Looks like you and

Nero are our best bet. Make sure that the woman and kids are not hurt. Go for it!"

Randy could not recall a situation that was more daunting. He knew that the life of the mother and three kids was squarely in his hands. He gathered up Nero and made his way to the rear of the Brewster home. The officers guarding the rear of the home nodded to Randy as he reached the back door of the home. Randy had one of his fellow officers pick the lock. He petted and reassured Nero as they moved slowly through the first floor. He did not want Nero barking or making any sounds that would alert the two thugs upstairs.

The veneer was wearing off the two thugs. Things hadn't gone as smoothly as anticipated. They were beginning to snap at each other. Each blamed the other for their predicament. Audrey Brewster picked up on the tension. She was genuinely frightened for the welfare and safety of her children. Moreover, she was unaware of where her husband was and if he was safe. She realized that she and her three children were at the mercy of these punks. Her fears were about to be allayed.

Randy eased Nero through the home's first floor. He could hear the two men arguing up above. He again reassured Nero. Randy was once again astonished at how Nero seemed to understand the situation and what the appropriate behavior was. Randy held fast, waiting to see what the thugs were going to do next. He knew that he couldn't wait too long to act. Not only were the mother and three children still in jeopardy, but Chief Benson and the Westfield Police Department officers on scene were unaware of what was going down inside the Brewster household.

Chief Benson had not given Randy a minimum amount of time. Randy knew, however, that the chief wouldn't wait long before sending in the troops. Randy once again reminded himself that the safety of Mrs. Brewster and the children was paramount. He could not even imagine the fallout that would follow a child bitten by a police dog. The determined dog handler crept softly with Nero until he reached a point that allowed him to see the entire second level of the Brewster home. Both of the thugs were in the middle bedroom with Audrey Brewster and her three children. He could hear the two continue to argue. One of them shouted at Audrey Brewster, telling her, "Shut the fuck up!" as she tried to calm her children.

Randy was becoming more and more worried that something bad was about to go down. The dog handler then decided on a course of action. He secured Nero at the top of the stairs landing with a long leash. He knew that the two thugs arguing so loudly enabled him to secure Nero without tipping them off. The behavior of the two thugs continued to a point where Randy had to act. All of his instincts told him that despite the intrinsic danger, he had to move. He took a deep breath, looked at Nero, and crashed through the door.

The Brewster foursome, completely traumatized by the entire affair, stared with disbelief as Randy Thompson kicked in the bedroom door. Equally astonished, the two thugs hesitated for a split second before springing into action. They both lunged at Randy, who proceeded to throw the first one through the bedroom door, directly into the waiting jaws of Westfield's only police dog!

Randy easily subdued the second thug and slapped him in cuffs. He then commanded Nero "OUT," which is the command to let go of the second man. Nero hesitated momentarily, not wanting to release his grip on the man's leg. Randy repeated the command "OUT." Nero immediately released his bite. Randy lavishly praised Nero, who retained a watchful eye on the shaken man.

Randy then radioed to the officer's surrounding the Brewster home, "Code 4," which signaled that the situation was neutralized. A group of Westfield Police Officers arrived within 15 seconds. Randy then turned his attention to Audrey Brewster and her three children. Audrey and the children were not harmed – at least outwardly. The mental trauma would be difficult to overcome. Audrey Brewster hugged her shaken children. She looked at Randy, a calm Nero at his side. She tried to mouth a thank you. She could only nod. Randy nodded back and briefly hugged her. She knew that she would never forget him and his dog.

Randy and Nero received a standing ovation when he exited the Brewster home. The chief was the first to shake Randy's hand. Chief Benson felt confident enough to gently pet Nero, who recognized the boss. The chief said, "I cannot tell you how proud we are of you and Nero. You have absolutely astonished everyone here in Westfield." Randy thanked the boss, telling the chief that the real hero was Nero.

Randy then heard a familiar voice call out to him from behind. He turned to see Carol Moore standing there. "Hello, Carol, what brings you out at this time of the night"

She replied that she couldn't sleep. "I always keep my police scanner on. When I heard this incident going down, I grabbed my keys and headed right on over. You and Nero are turning into quite an act." He and Carol agreed to meet for dinner the following evening.

Randy once again enjoyed having dinner with Carol Moore. A reasonable amount of time had elapsed since Sue Thompson had been taken from Randy. Carol recognized that he would need more time to let his wounded heart fully heal. Randy enjoyed this time with Carol. "Nice to be able to visit without a bunch of cops and bad guys around, isn't it?"

She smiled and said, "Yes, it really is."

Randy and Carol spent the remainder of the evening getting better acquainted. Carol revealed that she had never been married. She had been engaged four years prior. She told Randy her fiance had been killed two days before their wedding. He had immediate empathy with Carol. He held her hand as her eyes welled up with tears. Nothing else was said between them until they headed for their vehicles. They hugged before saying goodnight. Carol and Randy parted knowing full well that they very well that they would, in time, become more than just friends.

Westfield ISD Superintendent Fred Robinson greeted Randy and Nero three days after the Brewster incident. The Brewster incident was splashed all over the Westfield Times front page as well as on local TV outlets. The superintendent wanted to shake Randy's hand, but thought better of it. Police dog handlers do not want people unfamilar with their dogs to pet them.

Randy recalled a lecture by Harvey Rhodes during his training at Southern Training Academy. The instructor had spoken for several moments: "Dogs, like most animals, possess an intuitive sense which is underestimated by most folks. We have all looked at a person and thought that we don't like the looks of that person. He or she may be the most benevolent person in the world, but to you don't like their looks." Harvey hesitated for effect, then continued. "You will be amazed by how much your dogs can deduce on their own. Remember this, you and you alone are responsible for your dog. Be very careful when in proximity to people."

Fred Robinson introduced Randy and Nero to the assembly. The students applauded, obviously impressed by this police officer and striking German Shepherd. Randy thanked the assembled students. Many of whom had heard the previous assembly. He then proceeded to deliver a 10-minute lecture on police dogs in general, as well as an explanation of the Narcotic Detector Dog Program. The students listened intently as Randy explained how narc dogs are trained. The students asked a number of questions that indicated a genuine interest. One student asked Randy how Nero could sit quietly beside him as he lectured and answered questions. Mr. Robinson reluctantly interrupted, apologizing and telling the assembly that they had to move on. Randy then explained how the narcotic detector demonstration would go. Nero performed the standard suitcase exercise flawlessly. Randy thanked the assembly and encouraged them to perhaps consider police dogs as a career.

Chapter 7

Randy and Nero returned to work that evening. As usual, he received a number of congratulations from fellow officers. As usual, Randy was greeted by a series of barks and catcalls from fellow officers. Randy thanked the guys, many of whom had given sincere praise.

He hit the road with Nero, ready for whatever came their way. He was anxious to concentrate on the growing drug problem. He thought again of the recent Brewster episode. The Brewster episode would not have gone down except for Derrick's drug habit. The insidious nature of drugs had always baffled Randy. The thought of smoking, snorting, or injecting something into his body repulsed him.

Randy's ruminations were interrupted by dispatch. A Westfield patrol officer had pulled over an SUV for a routine lane change violation. The driver of the SUV was weaving in and out of traffic while driving through Westfield. The patrol officer lit up the SUV, which immediately pulled over. The Westfield officer approached the SUV from the rear, per routine police practice. The officer smelled the odor of marijuana wafting from the vehicle. He radioed dispatch to request Randy and Nero be dispatched to the scene. The handler/dog team arrived at the scene in about five minutes.

The patrol officer informed Randy that he had smelled the presence of marijuana emanating from the SUV. Randy recommended that the officer should remove the driver and the woman from the vehicle. The officer would indicate that he smelled the presence of marijuana. The officer then asked the driver for permission to search the vehicle. The driver refused. The officer then signaled for Randy and Nero to search the SUV for narcotics. Randy adrdessed the driver and his female companion and informed them that the patrol officer smelled marijuana, which established probable cause. The driver protested, saying that a police officer could not possibly smell marijuana. The officer just looked at the driver.

The vehicle was facing north. A moderate wind was blowing out of the north. Dog handlers are taught to always commence the search of a vehicle at the bottom of the wind. This tactic allows the narcotic detector dog the benefit of searching towards the "source," or location of the illicit drug. Randy approached the SUV, stopping approximately two paces from the vehicle. He then petted Nero before showing him the ball. Nero immediately launched into a frenzy, chomping at the bit, wanting to commence the search. Many, many folks mistakenly assume that the narcotic/detector dog like the narcotics. Nothing could be further from the truth. Illegal drugs mean two things to a narcotic detector dogs: Pleasing his/her master, and getting to play with the hard rubber ball!

Nero commenced a systematic search at the rear of the SUV. Randy had Nero check all of the possible points of the vehicle where odors of organic matter could escape. Nero checked the trunk seams, wheel well, and door seams on the right side of the vehicle. Randy had Nero check the engine compartment next. It was when Nero began checking the left side of the vehicle that the dog's behavior began to change. Animal psychologists refer to it as a "change in behavior." Randy recalled Harvey Rhodes explaining that when a drug dog smells even the slightest trace of marijuana or other illegal drugs, its brain is triggered by a chemical reaction that tells it that he is getting closer to the source, and the ball.

Randy noticed a gradual change in Nero's behavior as the German Shepherd searched the left side of the SUV. The dog stopped as it approached the fuel tank door. Nero stopped at the small door, sniffed several times, then tilted his head quizzically before looking at Randy. Nero was manifesting what is referred to as a "peculiar" alert. A peculiar alert or response occurs when a dog encounters a scent that smells similar to, or is positioned in proximity to a narcotic. Many narcotic detector dogs have manifested a peculiar alert when searching for narcotics in a room containing a concentration of legal drugs. Nero then scratched vigorously at the fuel refill door.

Randy encouraged Nero, who was now frantically scratching and biting at the fuel door. Nero looked at Randy, who grabbed the ball from his pouch and bounced it. The big dog was chewing on the ball as Randy told the patrol officer and shift sergeant that narcotics were hidden in the gas tank. The officer and shift sergeant looked quizzically at Randy. The dog handler didn't hesitate in telling the two Westfield officers that some type of narcotic was hidden in the gas tank. The shift sergeant asked Randy what they should inform the occupants that their vehicle was being impounded to facilitate a search of the vehicle's gas tank.

A city tow truck towed the SUV to the Westfield Police vehicle garage. The occupants refused to grant permission. Randy called Judge Harper, the county judge. Protocol dictated that the senior police official would normally call the judge to request a search warrant. However, given the specialized field, it was necessary for the dog handler him/herself to personally brief the judge. This process was essential should a drug bust end up in a trial. The prosecution will always call the dog handler to testify. His/her credentials and experience will validate the bust/arrest.

The on-duty mechanic removed the SUV's gas tank with little difficulty. The gathering of police officials stared in amazement upon seeing the gas tank. The tank had been welded into two compartments – one for gasoline and one for cocaine! After draining the gasoline from the tank, the mechanic pried open the remainder of the tank. The color drained from the faces of the faces of the two occupants as the mechanic removed approximately 25 kilos of pure cocaine. The patrol officer advised the two of their rights. Randy returned to headquarters to write his report. Nero was becoming accustomed to performing his assigned tasks, then returning to headquarters while his master completed paperwork.

The shift sergeant joined Randy in the training room. The sergeant asked Randy how the heck a dog could possibly differentiate between the odor of gasoline and cocaine. Randy did his best to explain to the sergeant the dogs' phenomenal olfaction capacity.

"Professionals to this day argue about how strong the dogs' olfaction ability is. I have personally observed German Shepherds pick up the scent of a human intruder well over 300 yards." Randy continued after pausing for a few seconds. "My canine instructor, Harvey Rhodes, told the class that he witnessed a German Shepherd narcotic detector dog locate one marijuana seed in a military barracks."

The shift sergeant was truly impressed by what Randy told him.

"Sarge," said Randy, "statistics are fine. Dog handlers, as a rule, don't worry about how strong a dog's olfaction is. We trust our dogs, whether it is one yard away or buried under anything! Nero and his kind will find the bad guy and his drugs."

The two SUV occupants adamantly refused to reveal whom they were working for. Randy briefed Chief Benson, Mayor Johnson, and several city council members on the growing drug problem.

"Taking out Ernie Olsen barley disrupted their operation," Randy answered several questions from the brass.

Chief Benson then interjected his opinion. Of course, his was the one that mattered. "We have discussed the problem with Randy. He will be relieved from his 8PM – 4AM shift. He will now be on his own with Nero. He'll be reporting directly to me." Chief Benson's commitment to Randy and Nero were total validation to the drug suppression program.

Randy's next major assignment took him away from Westfield to the county prison. Warden Ed McIntire had contacted Chief Benson, requesting help with a drug problem – not with inmates, but with his staff. The chief immediately agreed. Warden McIntire explained to the chief that strong rumors existed regarding staff use of various illicit drugs. Moreover, the warden was convinced that security officers were dealing drugs to inmates. Warden McIntire assured Chief Benson that the search would be confined to the employee locker area. Chief Benson asked the warden if the prison still had it's own drug dog. The warden replied, somewhat sarcastically, "Yes, Chief, we do. Unfortunately, he's part of the problem."

Chief Benson and the warden agreed that Randy and Nero would travel up to the county prison the following Monday morning.

Warden McIntire met Randy and Nero approximately one mile from the prison. The warden briefed Randy on the problem at the county prison.

"Randy," said the warden, "we are convinced that a sizeable number of the guards are dealing drugs with the inmates. You will search the staff locker rooms. You don't have to worry about the prisoners."

Randy assured the warden that he and Nero would do the best they could. Randy followed the warden back to the prison. The warden had directed his assistant to watch the employee locker room until he, Randy, and Nero arrived. He and his assistant were the only ones aware of the impending shakedown.

The security officers at the main gate were not overly concerned when the warden's vehicle approached, followed by Randy's Westfield black and white with an impressive German Shepherd riding shotgun. They assumed that the purpose of the visit was to shake down some inmates. The ruse worked perfectly. Warden McIntire escorted Randy and Nero directly to the employee locker rooms. Two male employees were ordered out of the dressing room. Word would spread like wildfire through the prison guards. McIntire wasn't concerned.

The locker room was enormous. The prison employed 178 people. Of that total, 140 were guards. Warden McIntire was confident that the problem was confined to guards. The warden told Randy that it was inconceivable that any state, federal, county, or local jail didn't experience some difficulty with guard behavior. The warden continued, "Our information tells us that it is really rampant here, Randy. We have to clean up this mess. I've been pleading with the county to authorize funds for a new drug dog. They say that the problem isn't that serious. I hope that your visit can change some minds." That said, they headed out to the employee locker room.

The deputy warden greeted them at the entrance. Two employees had been turned away by the deputy warden. The warden and deputy warden stood by the two doors as Randy and Nero commenced searching. Randy cut Nero loose to perform what is called a "scan." Scans are only performed in a totally controlled arena. Nero moved about the locker room in an ad hoc manner, seemingly confused. Randy knew better. Nero was not confused. He was attempting to pinpoint the specific location of several "sources." To an experienced handler it was a clear indication of multiple sources. Randy hitched up Nero to his leash and commenced a systematic search of the employee lockers. Nero responded to 21 employee lockers. Randy had written down the lockers numbers before completing the search.

The county prison lockers were controlled by a numerical combination lock. The prison administration retained a roster of the locker combinations.

Since a certified narcotic detector dog had responded to those lockers, which were owned by the county, no warrants were required. 17 of the 21 lockers contained illegal nartotics. Those drugs included crack cocaine, meth, and heroin. The on-duty officers utilizing one of the 17 were called in, interviewed, Mirandized, and sent home. Off duty officers were ordered to report to prison administration ASAP. They too would be interviewed, Mirandized, then sent home. All would face due process regarding their positions. Moreover, prison investigators would shake down inmates in an attempt to build a case against the 17 officers. Randy and Nero's work was done.

As he and Nero prepared to depart, Warden McIntire informed Randy that he would probably be called to testify at a later date. As Randy was shaking hands with the warden, McIntire asked Randy about the four lockers that Nero had responded to where no drugs were found. "Those lockers," Randy told the warden, "were next to lockers that contained narcotics." Finally, Randy informed the chief that all four were downwind from lockers with drugs.

Randy reported to the chief immediately upon his return to Westfield. Chief Benson greeted Randy with a very ebullient salutation.

"Good job, Randy," chortled the chief. "Warden McIntire called me immediately after you left. The rank and file guard corps was in chaos. Off duty officers involved were trickling in, unaware of what awaited them. Once again, you did us proud."

Randy thanked the chief, assuring the boss that he was happy to be supporting the Westfield PD.

Epilogue

Randy and Nero continued to impact the drug traffic in and around Westfield. The collective work of the handler/dog team changed the face of crime in Westfield. Randy's life had undergone a cataclysmic change. He had lost his wife to a criminal, but he had helped bring to justice the individual. He had gained an even stronger appreciation of the law. Finally, he had Nero to help him through the grieving process. He had met a woman, Carol Moore, in whom he believed he could find solace. He looked forward to the future.